A TALE OF TWO HEROES

AND OTHER SHORT STORIES

by

EDWYN PETERSEN

To Barb - To someone who is making a difference - Enjoy

First printed in 2005 10 9 8 7 6 5 4 3 2 1

The Publisher:
Edwyn Petersen
Suite 384, 300-8120 Beddington Blvd. N.W.
Calgary, AB T3K 2A8
E-mail: edpetersen@telus.net

Library and Archives Canada Cataloguing in Publication

Petersen, Edwyn, 1934-
A tale of two heroes : and other short stories / by Edwyn Petersen.

ISBN 0-9738363-0-X

I. Title.

PS8631.E826T34 2005 C813'.6 C2005-903413-0

Editorial: Gayl Veinotte
Copy Editing: Jennifer Keane
Cover Design: Robert Weidemann
Text Design: Heather Markham
Printing: Webcom

CONTENTS

Preface

Why write short stories about life in our school systems? If you're a student now, your world is largely regulated by the requirement to show up for classes every day and to do the work your teachers assign you, and that puts a big dent in the time you have for your friends and the rest of your real life. You know all there is to know about school and teachers. How can anyone tell you anything new about the place you live in every day, and how could short stories about school and teaching be interesting enough to read? Perhaps by dealing with some of the real problems people face in school every day?

If you're the parent of a small child or children, the school system looms large in your thoughts, mainly in terms of lunches made or forgotten, and buses to catch and schedules to keep. Underlying all the fuss of getting the kids off to school each day are all those concerns that you hope are being addressed: their safety and security, the relevance of what they are learning and how well school is equipping them to live successfully in society. Sometimes those concerns surface and you feel a twinge of apprehension. Perhaps it's justified. How can you tell?

If you work there and carry work home every night to grade and mark, you know how inadequate your resources are to meet all the needs you see in your students every day: the learning problems you cannot adequately address, the social problems you suspect but cannot identify and the crises which arise, for which trained staff are required but are not there because they could not be funded in this year's budget. Maybe next year. In the mean time, could you do a little more coaching in the next semester?

Why write short stories about life in our school systems? For the same reason we write about being in love, or about crimes that shock us, or about lives we can never live except in our fantasies. These stories show us something new in a world that seems so mundane.

Acknowledgements

Many people helped with the writing of this book. I am much indebted to Bev and Dianne Pamenter, who read an early rough draft and made useful and very welcome suggestions for its improvement. Harry and Iris Minifie were invaluable sources of information. Harry, in particular, drew on his knowledge and skill as a former wildlife officer in northern Saskatchewan to vet my references to wildlife in that area. Ron and Judy Petersen both gave freely of their time, advice and expertise in editing several selections. From his long experience both as a police officer and administrator, Ron was able to offer valuable insights into criminal behaviour and police procedures, both of which feature prominently in several stories. George Parry grew up on a reserve in Alberta and freely shared with me his own familiarity with Native ceremonies, beliefs and traditions to help me understand how a non-Native person unfamiliar with those same beliefs and traditions might struggle to fit in as a new teacher on a remote reserve. His insights were enlightening, and I hope the respect I gained from him for Native traditions and heritage are adequately portrayed in my writing.

I am pleased to have had two fine editors to work with during the writing of this text. Jennifer Keane walked me through my initial editing and showed me the errors of my ways, more times than I care to remember. The text is much improved as a result of her skill, patience and hard work. Gayl Veinotte worked with me on story ideas and on presentation. Her own skill as a published author and very busy writing coach was invaluable. My grateful thanks to both of them for hanging in there with me.

My wife did more than just listen to my frustrations at the tedium of the endless revisions and editing of my work. Betty worked as a nurse on a remote reservation in northern Saskatchewan. She knew from first hand experience about the conditions and problems that plague some reserves and how those conditions can impact the lives of the people who live there. She read and re-read my work, encouraging and supporting me as I shaped and developed the stories I wanted to tell. I owe her much and thank her sincerely.

INTRODUCTION

Welcome to a refreshing look at life in society's most undervalued profession. The stories in this series are all works of fiction, and they are all set in our local school system. None of the characters in these short stories are real people, but the themes explored here are certainly real: they're familiar to us from television newscasts and the headlines in our local newspapers.

You may remember your years in school as challenging and exciting or as the longest and most tediously boring interlude in your life. However you remember your school experience, it was a significant part of your life. Important and sometimes frightening things were going on around you when you were a child in school — things from which you were carefully shielded.

Nothing happens in society that does not also happen to the people, children and adults, who make up the school system of your province or state. They just don't happen very often in your own neighbourhood. When something significant does happen in a school you are familiar with, it seems like an anomaly, something quite unusual and astonishing, like a meteor falling from the sky. But meteors fall to earth all the time. If they don't often fall into your own back yard, it only means they're raining down somewhere else.

That is the premise of this book. The fictional stories presented here are the mirror image of real life situations in the larger educational system, of which your local school is only a very small part. They're funny or heartbreaking, tragic or uplifting: stories of life and death, and yes, even of the predators who occasionally haunt the halls of quiet little schools, just like the one your children may now be attending.

These stories take place for the most part, outside the classroom. They are all set during the Christmas break because that is usually the longest break in the school year. But this is not a book of Christmas stories. This is a collection of stories about students and adults dealing with serious issues, all of which arise from their connection to the school system.

The Christmas concert was a traditional feature of the school system until very recently, and it's still found in some systems. An alternative celebration such as a Winter Fest or Drama Presentation is often held to coincide with the end of the first term in order to end the term on a festive note. The Christmas concert has been revived here to serve as a backdrop for two of these stories.

I've tried to peal away the thick skin that hides the real life below the placid surface of your local school system. You'll relate to many elements in these stories, and the situations my characters find themselves in will be very familiar to many of you.

Enjoy.

Edwyn Petersen

The Day They Fired Santa

Large city schools don't have janitors. They have custodial services. When the teacher puts out the lights and locks the classroom door at night, the garbage can may be overflowing, the blinds hanging haphazardly, the chalk dust thick enough to write your name in—the room in general may look like a war zone—but it really doesn't matter. Before morning the gnomes of the custodial service will creep in and sanitize the place and it will look as good as new when the lights go on for the next day of class. The workers may be long-time school board employees who have cleaned the school and taken care of the building for years, or perhaps the cleaning contract has been "outsourced" to the lowest bidder, and the people who clean and tidy the room may not even know the name of the school they're cleaning and wouldn't care if you told them. If the system is big enough, efficiency may dictate how cleaning and maintenance will be done.

But small schools usually have janitors. Meadowvale Elementary is a small school on the edge of a small town in rural Alberta, and

Abe Henderson is Meadowvale's janitor. He's been there for years. The kids all know him, and he probably knows the name of every kid in the school. There's no mystery about who keeps the school clean and tidy at Meadowvale. Abe is always there to clean up or do whatever needs to be done, quietly, without anyone having to tell him what to do and usually without anyone noticing the work he does.

No one ever invites Abe to Meadowvale's special events, like the little graduation ceremony when the students move on to the composite high school on the other side of town. He's always there to clean up afterwards, of course, but over the years he has contributed his part to their education just as surely as if he were one of their teachers. From him little kids learn about the care of lawns and trees and growing things, and that hanging up snowsuits makes them dry for going home at night. Some kids see more similarity between him and their own parents than they do between their parents and the teachers who peer down at them over the piles of books and papers on their desks. He does real things, like their dads do. If a locker gets stuck, they call Abe to open it. If a toilet gets plugged, he unplugs it. And when a mouse gets into a classroom and the teacher calls for someone to come and chase it out, Abe shows up with his broom to stomp and swish about until the little critter heads out the door and the kids have giggled themselves silly.

It was late in December now, and Abe had been outside for well over an hour, digging out the small snow blower so he could clean off the school's walkways before the kids arrived for school. He shovelled steadily, working at his own methodical pace. His big black beard was covered in frost from his own breath, his whole body shrouded in his drab green snowmobile suit. When he had cleared enough of the snow, he opened the shed doors and pulled the snow blower out onto the walk. He started it, put it in gear and began his noisy round of the school's walks, the blower sending a steady stream of snow left or right as he directed the flow.

By the time he finished, most of the town kids had walked to school, and the rural kids were pouring out of the big yellow buses. He was dusted with snow from head to foot, and his big black beard was as white as the rest of him. A few of the older kids called out a greeting and he responded with a wave. He grinned at the little kids who giggled as he passed, calling him "Mr. Frosty" or "Mr. Snowman" or some such nonsense. He liked the kids and he was pleased when they noticed him. He could talk to little kids. It was talking to adults that made him nervous.

The Christmas break would start this week. He didn't get the full two weeks off that everyone else got, but he looked forward to the holidays as much as anyone. Not that spending the holidays alone was any great treat, but Hazel and Dan had invited him to spend Christmas with them on their farm again, and he thought he would go this year.

Abe had been working in his shed on Saturday morning when Hazel called. It took him a second to realize it was his phone that was ringing and he hurried in to pick it up before it stopped.

"Hello?"

"Hi, Abe. It's Hazel. How are ya? Haven't heard from ya in a dog's age. You keepin' good?"

With the first words she spoke he could feel his spirits lift. He had been feeling a bit down lately and he grinned broadly as he pulled up a chair to sit down for a phone visit. Nobody ever called Abe, so, when the phone rang he always feared it would be bad news. But Hazel was never bad news.

"Yuh. Yuh, I'm real good. Busy you know, but good. You get much of this snow down your way?"

That's how it always started. The news and then the weather, just like on television.

"How're you keepin'?" he asked. "And Dan? He's okay too? Lots of work now with the boys away, I guess, eh? Harry and Vincent coming home for the holidays?"

"Dan's good. Harry's comin' home, but not Vincent. It's too far to come with the baby, and Chrissie thinks they should stay home for Christmas and come out in the summer. Besides, they jack up the price of the flight from Toronto over the holidays, so it's not worth it for just a few days. It makes more sense to plan a visit for a week or two in the summer. But we'll miss them. So," Hazel asked, "what're you up to now?"

And as quickly as that they had exhausted the topics of conversation between them, but not the good wishes. From this point on the conversation would be a bit of a challenge because nothing much ever changed in Abe's life and he was becoming more remote from his sister and her family with each passing year. Abe tried to think of something to say to keep his end of the conversation up, but what was there to tell her? They had a new principal at school and he mentioned her in passing, but that was about it. They fell silent and he was afraid Hazel would say goodbye and be gone for another few months. Suddenly, he felt very alone and wanted her to keep talking a while longer.

"So, look Abe, if you're not doing anything special for Christmas, how be you come out to the farm? There'll only be Dan and Harry and me, and you know you'll be fine with us."

Hazel didn't have to finish the thought. She was referring to the last visit he'd made to Wilma's place and how upset he'd been by it. Abe grimaced involuntarily. That was five years earlier, but he could still hear his older sister making a joke of his stutter, as though he could turn it on or off when it suited him. She knew he didn't do well in crowds and yet she'd invited a whole bunch of people for dinner—one woman in particular she was trying to pair him up with. The more she pushed, the more he withdrew, but she wouldn't stop. Slowly, conversation died around them as Wilma kept asking him questions to prompt some dialogue between him and this neighbour she wanted him to meet. He stammered for a bit and suddenly his stutter came back, and then she was finishing sentences for him, just like she had when they were kids. He was so flustered he couldn't even excuse himself properly from the table. He stuck it out to the end of the meal, but when several men got up to go outside for a smoke, he went with them. He picked up his bag and grabbed the keys to Art's pickup from the hook by the door and peeled out of the yard. He left the truck at the bus station, the keys locked in the glove compartment. He figured he'd call from the bus station to tell Art where his truck was, but there was no time. When he got home he called Wilma, but Art answered and said she didn't want to talk to him, and he'd already gone and picked up his truck.

"You still there, Abe?" Hazel asked.

He had been quiet for a while, and her voice startled him.

"Yeah, I'm still here. I don't know Hazel, about coming for Christmas, I mean. I'll have to think about it," he said, already dismissing the offer in his mind.

"Hang on a bit. Dan wants to say hi."

Abe heard a bit of chatter; then Dan came on the line.

"Hello, you skinny old buzzard. How the heck are ya? You gonna come down here and spend some time with us over Christmas, so Hazel can fatten you up some?"

There was warmth in Dan's voice, in his friendly, insulting banter that only men who know and like each other well can offer and accept. He laughed quietly, trying to think of a good comeback, when Dan broke in and carried on.

"Look Abe, I really want you to come. We want to see you, and I have a job I could sure use your help with. I mean that. I picked up an old binder at an auction a while back. I want to get her up and running and donate it to the pioneer exhibit at Kindersley. Not just paint and varnish. I want her to look like new, but she's got to be in good working order so they can put on demonstrations with her for the tourists. It's an old McCormick Deering, you know. Hazel thinks your dad had one, or one like it, when you were growing up. Does that ring a bell with you?"

Abe was hooked immediately. "Yuh, that rings a bell, all right. You ever try to set up the twine-tying part, the knotter, on one of them old beasts? That can be a real bearcat of a job. And if this one's been sitting in a shed for fifty years or more..."

Miles away, on the other end of the line, Dan cuddled Hazel and kissed her on the forehead. Covering the mouthpiece so Abe couldn't hear, he grinned and said, "Asking old Abe to come because you care about him and want to see him is like trying to drag a mule out of a burning barn. But give him a chance to work at a really interesting job and he knows you respect him, and he needs that. He'll come. You'll see."

Abe replayed the conversation in his mind as he dry-mopped the long hall of the school on Monday morning. His step was light and he felt good. He'd spend Christmas with Hazel and Dan, and it would be a good visit.

The kids were making decorations, and little bits of paper were everywhere. The garbage cans were filling up fast and the recycle bins were overflowing by lunchtime. He moved chairs and tables, packed up bags of waste paper, brought down boxes of stored decorations for the tree and mopped the hallways three or four times that day. Being janitor was always a full-time job, and to Abe, just before the holidays, it seemed there was twice as much work to do. But there was a job to come that he actually looked forward to—playing Santa for each of the parties in the lower grades. He would make a brief appearance in the joint kindergarten/grade-one room and in each of the grades from two to four. By grade four, the kids were getting a bit past it and they knew who he was, but it was tradition, and he'd make an appearance for them. At least for them he didn't have to wear the big white beard over his own wild whiskers. The kids loved his visits, and so did he, although you would never have guessed it from his gruff manner.

Before Santa's visits to the classrooms, of course, Santa would make his appearance at the concert on Thursday night, before the last day of school. Abe always came running down the wide centre aisle and rushed up onto the stage. There was only one hall in town larger than the school's gym, so weddings, the occasional funeral and gatherings of all sorts took place in the gym, and the modest facility fee paid his overtime and constituted a slush fund that the school could use for little extras, like the Christmas treats for the kids. He'd have a sack of mini chocolate bars or those foil-covered chocolate coins in little string sacks, and the teachers would write the name of every kid on a piece of paper and attach it with tape to a large candy cane. Those had to be given out by grade, of course, but he could toss out the candies, and everybody got a charge out of the scramble.

For such a quiet and retiring man, it was a wonder that Abe put on such a convincing performance. He would ask all the kids if they had been especially good that year, and when they all yelled out their answers, some kids, usually in grade five or six, would call out, "No," loud enough for everyone to hear. He would freeze, turn slowly to the audience and say something like, "Did you hear what I heard?" Then he would single out one of the kids who had said the loudest "No" and call him or her, although it was rarely a girl, to come up on stage to sit on Santa's knee and explain himself. It didn't matter what the kid said. The parents and teachers, not to mention the kids themselves, would have a ball. The kid he singled out would always agree to be a good boy or girl for Christmas, and Abe would give him a special treat that he had paid for himself—a large chocolate bar or a big bag of chocolate coins.

But this year he would call up Lucy Korszinski, the new principal, and have a bit of fun with her. She seemed like a good sport, and he was sure she would ham it up like a pro. She had only been at the school since September, and the people would want to see her get roasted, just a bit. And it would be just a bit; he was sensitive about people's feelings and would be very careful not to offend her or cause her embarrassment. Abe was thinking about the surprise that would show on her face when he called her, chuckling to himself as he walked home for supper that evening.

Evelyn Boychuck was also thinking about supper on the family farm just outside of town, as she did every evening at about five. She and Kirk had been married for fifteen years. They had three children: Robby in the composite high school, and two in the elementary school, a boy in grade five and a girl in grade three.

They had been very much in love when they got married. Kirk had always been a quiet man, not much given to showing his feelings, and at first they had been so busy building a life together that she had been content with just his presence and his support. But that was changing for Evelyn. There had been romance before they were married, but there was none in their marriage now, and she keenly resented that void in her life.

Evelyn's church sponsored a number of good social programs. She helped out with the local food bank and Kirk did too, but it didn't appeal to her as much as it did to Kirk. There was a foreign outreach program supported by local farmers, and Kirk was supportive of that initiative, as well. Farmers paid their own way to a foreign country torn by war or plagued by natural disasters to help other farmers in any way they could. They might take a load of hand tools to give to the people and stay to work with them for as long as they could. One group set up a machine shop to keep local equipment running. Another group donated the equipment for an irrigation system and helped the local farmers set it up and learn to run it. Some were not even members of their church. They were just fine people, reaching out to help other farmers in need.

There were no end of good projects Evelyn could work on, and her help was always appreciated. Safe, worthwhile, socially respectable causes every one of them, and all of them as repetitious and predictable as her life had become.

Abe and Evelyn knew each other by sight, of course, but they lived in separate worlds. Abe had moved to the town about twenty years earlier. He lived alone in one of those tiny old houses you only see in small towns. He kept to himself. For a few years he had boarded with a family in town and worked at odd jobs, until the school janitor job came up. In some ways, he almost regretted buying his little house. He missed the company of the family he had boarded with. On the other hand, he had a place of his own, with his own lawn and garden, and a shed where he could putter about to his heart's content. For the most part he was content and self-contained, but he did get lonely from time to time.

When the urge to talk to someone simply overwhelmed him, he would go out and buy a little company. Abe was realistic. He had long since accepted that he would always be alone and he was okay with that. He was not a handsome man. He was not a rich man. People only shared company with you if you had something to offer them in exchange. He took stock of himself and decided, rightly or wrongly, that he had nothing to offer anybody. His house was too small to rent out a room, so he chose to live his quiet life alone, with one exception. He would wander down to the local grocery store and pick up a few things several times a week. That was how he purchased company. He could talk to a neighbour while selecting this or considering that at the grocery store.

He quickly discovered spending money was easy if you didn't know what you wanted to buy. Abe's solution was to buy paper products: boxes of tissues, paper towels and toilet paper. It made sense. He only came into the store hoping to run into someone he knew; he didn't spend a lot of money. He could have gone down and hung around the garage, but he looked at the three old men who already did that and felt uncomfortable at the thought of it. They had no reason for being there, and anyone could see that the operator would be just as glad if they shoved off. Eating in restaurants was expensive and, again, you don't meet people while you're eating at separate tables. Nope. The solution was paper towels and little snippets of conversation two or three times a week.

Evelyn Boychuck made an unscheduled stop at the grocery store this Tuesday evening about 8:00. She was in town to pick Robby up after his hockey game, and they stopped to get a carton of milk on the way home. She sent Robby in, and when he didn't come out after about ten minutes, she went in to see what the holdup was.

Robby had attended Meadowvale Elementary School for eight years and had known Abe for all of them. Robby was flying. It was his second year in minor hockey and he had just managed his first shutout. He was so pumped, he would have talked to a "happy face" if you'd drawn ears on it. His mother had shown little interest in his victory and hadn't even seemed to be listening to him. Perhaps she simply didn't understand hockey. More likely, when you wanted to talk about shots on goal, you needed to talk to a buddy, right? He saw Abe up by the checkouts and hailed him immediately.

Was Abe interested in his game? Sure, Abe was interested. He genuinely was. He warmed to the kid's enthusiasm. Well, there was the impossible shot, upstairs on the left, that Robby hadn't even seen, but gloved instinctively. Then the one like a rocket, probably sixty miles an hour coming right for the space between his skates, and he got that one by dropping to his knees and falling on it. Then there was a wicked shot, stick side, out of nowhere, and that dangerous one dribbling in behind him. He kicked that one out. He was...he did...it was...they were...and so on for a good five or ten minutes.

Robby confided to Abe that he wanted to make it all the way to the National Hockey League. He wanted to play goalie for the Flames. Or maybe the Oilers; he wasn't sure. Abe could only just identify most of the players he mentioned, but he smiled and nodded. Robby wanted to see his picture in Hockey News some day. He picked up a copy of the magazine from the rack and thumbed through to a classic shot of Gretzky skating victoriously with the Stanley Cup over his head. See, here was the picture, a man in uniform drenched with sweat, skating toward the camera. They held the magazine between them, Robby bursting with pride and Abe happy to be included in the boy's excitement.

That was all Evelyn saw as she spotted Robby with Abe in the store. Abe, the older man who lived alone, intent on their conversation; her son Robby, a fourteen-year old boy looking eagerly up at him, apparently sharing the excitement generated by a photo in a glossy magazine.

She didn't even stop to pick up the milk. She said nothing, but snatched the magazine and jammed it back into the rack. She froze Abe with a look of pure hatred, and he staggered back in amazement. Robby, shamefaced and quiet, assumed she was angry because he'd kept her waiting for a few minutes while he relived the game with Abe. He followed his mother off to the truck without a word.

She said nothing the whole way home. When Robby tried to start a conversation, she told him that she couldn't talk about it now, but she would settle with him later. He couldn't figure out why she was so angry. It seemed out of proportion to the crime he had committed, but that's parents for you. Sometimes they don't make a whole lot of sense to their kids.

As soon as Evelyn got home she called the chair of the local school board. Joan Blasetti was a neighbour Evelyn had known for years and a woman she could talk to easily. She didn't waste time on small talk. She had reason to suspect, she said, it was only a suspicion at this time mind you, but she felt strongly that a note of caution was warranted about the janitor of the Meadowvale School. No, she could not go into details, but she had seen an incident involving her son and the janitor that disturbed her. Not an overt act or anything illegal, but his attitude had been enough to concern her. As she said, it was only a suspicion, and Lord knows, she didn't want to accuse anybody without proof. But one needed to be careful, given the revelations about men "like that" coming out in the newspapers every day. Now, she wasn't accusing anybody of anything. It was just, well, perhaps we need to be a little more vigilant where the safety of our children is concerned.

Evelyn's call was very disturbing. Joan was in her third term on a board of education overseeing thirty-four schools in two counties, and to her knowledge, no situation like this had ever come before this board or any boards that had preceded it. But something had obviously upset Evelyn, upset her so badly, in fact, that she didn't want to discuss it over the phone, and she wasn't the kind of person who would make up a story like this.

Joan couldn't ignore Evelyn's call. Her first responsibility was to protect the children where Abe worked, and Evelyn was suggesting that he posed a threat to them. She didn't know what to do.

Her first impulse was to call the maintenance supervisor to inform him of Evelyn's accusation and have him suspend Abe immediately. She thought about it for a few minutes before deciding against it as too dramatic an action to take, given the vague nature of Evelyn's accusation. Firing, or even suspending, a worker was a serious business, and she didn't want to overreact. Besides, she wasn't even sure if she had the authority to act without consulting the other members of the board.

Probably it would make more sense to call a special committee meeting to review the charges without prejudging the man before they had heard the whole story. It would have to be after the holidays, of course, because a number of people would be away and no one would want to get into this until the new year. Besides, the school holiday started in just three days; surely they could muddle through until the kids were out of school. They would have to resolve this thing quietly after the holidays. The problem was what to do about Abe for the next three days.

If the call had been about a schoolteacher, Joan would never have called the principal of Meadowvale School. There was a process in place for dealing with complaints against teachers. She would have called the superintendent of education. He would have arranged a meeting with the teacher and the principal and a representative of the teachers' professional association, and the accusation would have been fully examined, with due regard for the rights of all parties.

But Abe Henderson wasn't a teacher. He was a janitor, an hourly worker who qualified for sick time and a paid vacation only because, even on his minimum salary, the law said they had to give it to him. There was no process in place to deal with this specific type of situation, at least none she knew of. Then again, Abe had been working at Meadowvale School for all these years and he had never caused a problem. So maybe the answer was just to put him under a little more supervision for the next three days and make sure he wouldn't be alone with the kids.

So Joan called Lucy Korszinski, the newly appointed principal at Meadowvale Elementary, to put her in the picture and to warn her, in the strictest confidence, that Abe should not be allowed near the children alone. Then she added that Mrs. Korszinski would have to ensure that he was properly supervised and that she personally would be responsible for making sure that no incidents occurred until they could decide what to do with Abe after the holidays.

When appointments are made to a teaching staff, they are almost always temporary for at least one year and often for several. The clear implication of what the chairperson told Lucy was that she could kiss her job goodbye if anything even remotely like a scandal occurred involving Abe Henderson, especially since she had been warned. Lucy didn't know Abe very well. She'd only been at the school for a little more than three months. To her, he seemed like a rough sort of person. He did not make friends easily and he did not go out of his way to appear particularly friendly either. He looked clean, but scruffy, and his beard gave him a sinister appearance that made it easy for her to imagine that he was capable of anything.

Lucy called a staff meeting for early Wednesday morning. She alluded to certain allegations that had come to her attention about Abe, which for reasons of confidentiality she could not divulge in detail. Her message to the staff was to watch him closely and not to allow him to be alone with, or get close to, any of the children. No close contact with the children, and absolutely no individual contact with any child without a teacher in the room. There was an awkward silence when one of the older teachers brought up the tradition of Abe coming into the classrooms as Santa on Friday morning, and appearing as Santa at the concert on Thursday evening. Lucy knew nothing about the Santa tradition, and she would have to think about how best to handle the situation. In the mean time she suggested they let Abe carry on as usual, but under close supervision.

A rumble of whispered conversation broke out following her announcement. It was a shock to all of them. They had all known Abe for so long, and to think he was "that sort of person" all these years! Well, you just don't know what he might have been up to, do you?

Lucy had warned them that these were merely unsupported allegations that they were required to keep confidential, but before the day was out, the suspicion was treated as fact and the "fact" was spread all over town. Meadowvale was not a large town and it was blessed with a very efficient telephone system.

Lucy sat at her desk idly playing with a pencil. She had been sitting there for the last two hours and had accomplished nothing. She would recommend to the board that Abe be fired for the good of the school, and as quietly as possibly. That was obviously what the chairperson wanted from her. She found the prospect distasteful because Abe, however odd he may have appeared to her, was a good worker and had apparently been a reliable and trustworthy employee for years. If she failed to file a suitable recommendation to fire Abe, she was unlikely to be confirmed in her position as principal for the next school year. Her job was on the line, as was her integrity.

It would be best done during the holidays, when it would cause the least disruption for the kids. He had no contract that bound the board to continue to employ him. There was a reason the board hired workers, paid them an hourly wage, and never gave them a contract of employment. Abe was expendable, as he was meant to be. He was also alone, with no family and no one to stand up for him or take his part.

At least Lucy would not have to fake an excuse to request his dismissal. With the gossip now swirling about him, his position in the school was so compromised that he couldn't work here any longer. She had taken at least a dozen phone calls this morning from parents concerned for the welfare of their children, now that Abe was under suspicion of some unspecified but highly improper contact with children. There were three more days of school before the holiday break, and they would be three very long and very difficult days.

Wednesday morning had started normally for Abe. He worked away, mopping and cleaning as the kids came in, and he shared a friendly chat with several teachers before they were called down for a brief staff meeting. But something must have happened overnight, because whatever they learned at the meeting had upset them, and most of them were preoccupied and too distracted to even talk to him. In fact, none of the teachers talked to him all day, and even the kids seemed to shy away from him as he worked. After lunch he was asked to leave his other work and start the thorough cleanup of one of the classrooms that would normally have been cleaned over the holidays. Mrs. Korszinski told him that they had changed class schedule to free the room up so he could have the rest of the day to work on it, and would he please stay there until it was finished. She told him to lock the door so none of the kids would wander in if they got confused by the change of rooms in the afternoon. It was a precaution, she said, because he would have all his cleaning chemicals in the room, and they had to be sure none of the kids could be exposed to them. There was something in the way she talked to him that was odd, and even Vera, the secretary, wouldn't look at him when he said hello to her.

The bell rang for dismissal at 3:30, and he went to the entrance where the bus kids were getting dressed to board the bus. He always liked to be on hand in case someone couldn't find a snow boot, or a locker got stuck or something, only tonight there were two extra teachers there already, and they said thanks, but they didn't need his help tonight. Something was wrong, but nobody was going to tell him what the problem was.

Abe worked quickly in the empty school, finishing his chores about an hour later than usual because of the extra work he had been asked to do. He felt uneasy as he locked up and headed home, and he dropped by the grocery store to pick up a few things and perhaps spend a few minutes chatting with some of his neighbours at the checkout. But even here, no one would look him in the face. No one would talk to him. The checkout girl giggled nervously when she rang up his items, and seemed reluctant even to touch the money he gave her.

The magazine rack caught his eye as he passed the girl, and instantly he remembered the look on Evelyn Boychuck's face when she had barged into the store the night before. In the rack behind where he and Robby had been talking were all the girlie magazines, and magazines for body builders with pictures on the covers of men with bulging muscles contorted into fantastic shapes. And he could put a name to that look now. He had never seen it in anyone's face before, but he knew what it was. It was revulsion, disgust, loathing. It was what you might feel for someone with a foul disease, someone who could infect your son by just touching him. His mouth went dry. Someone coughed behind him, and he realized that for several minutes he had been standing in the way of a line of people wanting to get by. And not one of them, not one of his neighbours would speak to him, if only to ask him to move out of the way. He was numb and sick as he walked home.

At school the next day, everyone was watching him. No one asked him to do anything in any of the classrooms. He was told to set the gym up for the concert that night, but other than that, almost no one spoke to him for the whole day. He went home at 4:30 for a little supper, but didn't feel much like eating. He was being frozen out, and he felt sure he knew why. By 5:30 he was back at the school, opening the doors and getting the place ready for the concert.

The parents and students came, the teachers organized their classes and the concert began. The audience was silent, as though they were in church or at a funeral. They clapped very quietly at the end of each performance, and suddenly it was time for Santa to make his appearance. Abe was in his borrowed suit and he made his rush down the aisle "Ho, Ho, Hoing" all the way. But you could have heard a pin drop. The children sat rigid, as if in formation. The parents did not look at him when he got up on stage. He tried to carry on with the usual, "Has everybody been good this year?" but only a few of the younger children answered him, and there were pronounced "shushes" from the older ones. The candy canes and chocolate coins were distributed in almost total silence. He limped to the conclusion of the performance, bewildered and sickened by his reception. He had intended to call Mrs. Korszinski down to sit on Santa's knee and tell everybody if she'd been a good girl all year. It was programmed into him, and though he could see it would be a disaster, he could not stop himself. Perhaps he needed confirmation of what he suspected. Perhaps he needed the final public humiliation because he had not been given the courtesy of a private disclosure of the accusations being made against him.

"Well, everybody seems to be real good this year. But what about little Lucy Korszinski?"

It should have brought the house down. There was an audible groan of embarrassment.

"Well, Lucy, you better come down and sit on Santa's knee and tell everybody if you've been real good all year."

Abe seemed frozen in place in the centre of the stage, a pathetic caricature of the happy fat man he was supposed to be portraying. No one moved. No one made a sound. After a moment he called out again, "Well, Lucy, maybe you come down and tell Santa why nobody talks to him when he's been real good for lots of years, eh?"

He was crying now. He was past hurt, past embarrassment. This was the kind of humiliation that destroys a man. It had come out of nowhere. It had a name, but no single face. He had not been accused, and he could not defend himself. But he was condemned, sentenced and dismissed. He did not belong here anymore. He was not a parent. He was not a teacher. He had no stake in this pageant, and their revulsion seemed to well up and choke him.

He walked to the steps at the end of the stage and sat down heavily. No one moved or spoke or seemed even to breathe. Mrs. Korszinski sat unmoving, like the rest of the audience. He looked over the sea of faces. He could put names to most of them. Many had been students in this school just ten or fifteen years earlier, and he had known them all their lives, as he now knew their kids. And the faces were all of stone.

At length, Mrs. Korszinski rose, came to the front of gym and turned to face the audience. "I want to thank all of the teachers and children for the wonderful songs and plays tonight. It is quite late and we still have school tomorrow, so this concludes our concert for this evening and this year. I wish you all a Merry Christmas and a Happy New Year, and may the coming year be a prosperous and productive one for all of us. Mrs. Gates, would you lead the kindergarten out, and would all the children go with their teachers back to their classrooms to remove their costumes and get dressed. Thank you all for coming. Parents, please go to the individual classrooms to pick your children up and, again, Merry Christmas."

The spell was broken. People stood up, put on coats and hats and filed quietly out of the gym. Santa sat alone on the top step, quietly sobbing into his great white cotton beard.

But Abe the janitor was as professional as any of them, if not more so. He got up, went back to the janitor's room, hung up the Santa costume, got out his big dry mop and went back into the empty gym. He walked up the centre aisle and down both of the side aisles, pushing the few bits of paper together to the bottom of the stage steps. He quickly brushed the stage over and gathered all the dust into the garbage can by the front door. The school was almost empty by the time he was finished, and he just continued on down the halls, one after another, until the whole building was ready for the morning.

When he came to the front office, Mrs. Korszinski was waiting for him. She seemed cold and impersonal, but she was an unwilling actor in this sudden crisis she had helped to create, and there was nothing she could do to stop it now. He saw this in her face, but he didn't blame her for what had happened.

"Mr. Henderson, I'm truly sorry for what has happened, but you know my hands are tied. The board is meeting tomorrow to consider whether you should continue as janitor here or be outplaced immediately."

Apparently, if you have a degree in school administration you don't say "fired," you say "outplaced.'" Abe was quite calm now. He knew what she meant, but he wanted to hear her say it out loud.

"What's happened, Mrs. Korszinski? What happened between last week and this week so I'm gonna be fired, eh? What? I leave the toilets dirty? Did I say something wrong to somebody? Did I sleep in and come late to school? What am I being fired for, Mrs. Korszinski?"

"The board will discuss your case tomorrow, Mr. Henderson. That is really all I know. You'll have to talk to the board secretary, Mr. Abernathy, about the details of the meeting. I understand, confidentially, that they have the utmost regard for your work, and I wouldn't be surprised if they offered you a very generous settlement. Perhaps two or three months' pay. But I advise you to say nothing and accept whatever they offer you. I think you know that, aside from two weeks' notice, they are not legally bound to offer you any settlement at all."

She means this, Abe thought. She's not unfriendly, and she's offering me what she thinks is good advice. She thinks two or three thousand dollars, and a man leaves behind his whole life, and everything.

"You think I'm dirty. You think I'd hurt the children. After fifteen years here, you think I would hurt one of the little ones? Why? Twenty years I lived in this town. I got a little house and neighbours, and nobody can say I ever did nothing wrong, 'cause I didn't. Never."

He was crying now, and Lucy wished she could comfort him, but what could she do? She was an employee, just like him. They would have to let him go. The community had made its feelings clear tonight. There would be no groundswell of support for him. No one in that audience had stood up for him tonight, and no one would tomorrow. He was a harmless little man who had been different for years. Now, suddenly, his very remoteness, his funny little habits, had caused him to be labelled a public danger, a threat to the children of the community. No one would risk contamination by defending him.

All this passed between them in a single look, and they both knew there was nothing more to say. She said good night and left him to lock up. He went back to the classrooms, checking each one, room by room. When school opened tomorrow there would not be one scrap of paper or one orange peel left for someone else to clean up. It was close to 9 o'clock when he finished. He stood in the hallway and said goodbye to the building. He had spent more time here in the last fifteen years than he had in his own little house. It was like a friend. He wanted to say goodbye properly. He didn't take the flag down, because there would be no one to put it up in the morning. He put the lights out and locked the doors for the last time. He took his coat and his spare pair of boots with him. He would not be coming back to get anything.

At home, he made a cup of tea and sat down to look at what was left of his life. He was going to be fired. She had said as much. He had a little pension, but not enough to live on. He was only fifty-five, far too young for the old-age pension and far too old for a new job. All he knew was how to look after a school and how to look out for little kids, and nobody was going to hire him to clean a school again. He could take unemployment for a few months, but that wouldn't last long. Even if he had enough money to live on, could he face living with people who would turn on you in a second, for nothing? He could try to sell his little house, but there were two others just like his for sale in town, and they hadn't sold in about a year. Anyhow, where was he to go after twenty years here?

He sat in the dark for a long time. He went back and forth in his mind over every option, and none of them were acceptable to him. Sometimes a person just gets tired. Sometimes the struggle to put one foot in front of the other is too great. The way seems too long, and anyway, it all comes down to the same thing in the end. Had he been married, this might never have happened, or at least there would have been someone to talk it through with. But there wasn't anyone to talk to. And he didn't want to call his sisters. What would he say to them?

He tidied up the little kitchen and put the dishes in the sink. He got his snowmobile suit from the hook by the back door and put it on. He took his hunting rifle from behind the door, went to his little shed out back and shot himself.

The phone rang just after he left the house, but he was already too far away to hear it. Dan let it ring five or six time before hanging up. Abe had finally agreed to spend Christmas with them on the farm, and Dan was calling to find out when Abe would be there. Hazel thought he must be working late at the school, but when she called an hour later, a stranger answered. Their conversation was brief. He identified himself as a police officer and confirmed that, yes, this was Abe's number, and then he asked who she was. She told him she was Abe's sister, and gave him her address and phone number. She asked what had happened, but she thought she already knew what he was going to say.

He told her as gently and as simply as he could. Abe was dead. It looked like he had shot himself. It might have been an accident, but they were still investigating and that was all they knew at this time. Hazel had only one other question: where had they found him? When the officer said he'd been found in the utility shed in the yard, her heart felt like a stone in her chest. She knew immediately it wasn't an accident, and she could guess why he was found in the shed. Abe wasn't one to leave a mess for someone else to clean up.

Hazel called Wilma later that evening to tell her about Abe, and Wilma was surprised by the news, but not overly touched by it. She and Abe had never really been close and they had not reconciled after the embarrassment he had caused on his last visit to her home. Wilma didn't attend the coroner's inquest either. She said it seemed unnecessary to drag things out now that he was gone. She did manage to accept her share of his tiny estate however, because, after all, he was her brother.

At the inquest, the coroner asked if anyone could suggest anything, any problem in Abe's life that would explain his suicide.

Hazel couldn't, and no one from the community could either, apparently. The coroner thought perhaps living alone had isolated Abe and made him prone to depression, and he expressed a sincere concern for all older people who are alone and isolated at Christmastime. There was nothing more to say or to do, so he completed his duties as quickly as he could and closed the file on Abe Henderson.

Christmas was a very quiet affair at the Boychuck farm that year. There were the usual presents, of course, and the traditional dinner, but the life had gone out of the celebration for all of them. Robby surprised his little brother Christmas afternoon when he hauled the big black tote bag full of all his hockey equipment up to his brother's room and gave it to him. He said he didn't want to play hockey anymore and left the bag sitting in the middle of the room. Kirk found a number of chores that needed his attention and spent a lot of time in the workshop; Robby worked closely with him for most of the holidays.

Evelyn knew what was happening, of course, but there was nothing she could do about it. Robby would have told his dad about the scene in the store over the magazine, and Kirk would have put the pieces together. It was a cold, lonely holiday, and she was glad when it was over. Her neighbour, Joan Blasetti, the chair of the school board, called early in the new year. Her term on the board was up that spring, and she didn't want to serve another term. Evelyn was well known in the community, and she would probably be elected if she ran for a seat on the board. And Joan offered to help her with her campaign, because they certainly needed someone on the board with Evelyn's strong commitment to duty and moral integrity.

Evelyn sat by herself in the kitchen, her coffee cold and untouched on the table before her. Perhaps she should run for the school board. It would give her something to occupy her time. It was obvious that Kirk would have very little need for her company from now on.

~

'Twas the Night Before Christmas...

The night was cold and raw, the temperature dropping as the wind picked up. The dusting of snow from earlier in the day was wind-whipped to pellets as hard as gravel. To those lucky enough to be warm and comfortable and inside tonight, the snow and the sudden cold snap were not unwelcome. The snow was the perfect backdrop that made the Christmas lights shine that much brighter against the darkness.

Not everyone, of course, was lucky enough to be inside enjoying family and friends this Christmas Eve. The police and the various emergency services were working or on standby, as they always were, regardless of the holidays. They did their work despite the weather, and while this was a miserable night, it was also Christmas Eve, and for most of them it was still a special time of the year. The social workers at the homeless shelters felt the warmth of the season and shared it with their clients. Even the volunteers walking the alleys, bringing soup and hot coffee to the hard cases who would not come in out of the cold, were constantly wished a Merry Christmas and a Happy New Year by people who hadn't the slightest hope of either. Good wishes are infectious at Christmas time, and a surprising number of people succumb to a mild case of goodwill toward their neighbours. And for a little while, at least, the future seems more promising and their troubles less burdensome.

There are exceptions to every rule, of course. To Vicky Penrose, the small figure huddled on the bench in the deserted park, as lonely and deserted as the park itself this evening, the weather was insignificant. Nor did she share any sense of goodwill or hope for the future. But the chaos of her emotions had subsided as she sat watching the river just a few yards away. An empty calm had enveloped her, and she let her mind drift with the effortless current.

The decision to end her life had formed of itself, without her conscious intention. It came slowly to her, and only when her confusion and humiliation gave way to a sense of emptiness did she recognize it for what it was: a dreadful calm, like that of a drowning man who accepts his death and slips beneath the waves when he's too tired to swim any longer. In that insidious peace, in the blink of an eye, a life of promise and infinite value can be refused.

She wasn't crying. She was all cried out. She'd started crying Friday morning just after her visit to the clinic, when the nagging fear had been confirmed. She'd suspected something was wrong for weeks, yet she couldn't bring herself to admit that she might be pregnant. But the doctor had confirmed it. She was pregnant, and there it was. Now it was Sunday night, Christmas Eve, and she was alone in this deserted park, waiting for the next step.

She was surprised that it had happened, really, getting pregnant. She had known Steve all her life. Their families attended the same church and they lived close enough so that they had always attended the same schools. They had played together as kids until they weren't kids any more. Then they began to treat each other with that degree of distance that separates kids as they become conscious of their own maturing sexuality.

Although they had been aware of each other all through elementary school and junior high, it was Steve who suddenly discovered Vicky all over again in senior high.

Suddenly and quite unexpectedly the relationship became vital to both of them. They spent hours on the phone, even though they were together the better part of the day at school. Steve had taken to hanging around her locker just to see her for a few minutes between classes. They would meet in the corridor between their classrooms or on the stairs leading to the language arts room or at the exit from the biology lab on Thursdays, when she had a class and he didn't. They would hold hands for a few minutes, then Vicky would send him off to his class or to study hall or to his locker or wherever, neither of them fully aware of how their relationship was changing.

When they were not in school, they followed much the same routine, with just as little thought or effort. She would ask him if he wanted to come over to study in the afternoon, as if it were a new idea, even though they were together every afternoon. And he would ask her if she wanted to go out on Saturday after work, as though either of them could have imagined doing anything on Saturday evening without the other. They were in love and they loved being together. They never talked about having sex. When it came, it was as natural as holding hands or kissing good night, and just as wonderful.

And now she was pregnant.

Who do you turn to when the whole framework of your life dissolves, and you can't pretend any longer? Your mom? It should have been natural. They had always been close, but when Vicky began to suspect about the baby, a gulf had opened between them, and now her mother seemed strangely distant from her. How could she face her when she found out about the baby? She couldn't talk to her mother.

Your father? How do you go to your father and say, "Hi Dad. Guess what? Your little girl's pregnant." Besides, her father had suffered a minor heart attack at work a few months earlier and was still on temporary sick leave until they could get his blood pressure down. She couldn't lay this burden on him, too. So Vicky had turned to Allison Myers, a girl she knew from school. A girl who had seen more of the ugly side of life than Vicky could ever have imagined and, strangely, someone she thought she could trust.

Vicky had known Allison all through junior high, but their friendship, if that's what it was, had started quite dramatically in high school one morning. Allison had arrived early at school because she had nowhere else to go. She was in the washroom trying to do something about the ugly bruise on her face—with Marty, of course, because they were always together—when the policewoman from the Community Relations Office in the school tracked her down to escort her to the principal's office. It had happened before, and everybody knew the story. Her dad was a drunk, and her home life was a mess. Her mother had called the police on more than one occasion to intervene in a family dispute. It must have been more serious this time because, according to Marty, Allison's mother had gone to the women's shelter with the two younger kids, and the police were holding her father on an assault charge.

They could stay in the shelter for the time being, but they would have to find a new place to live because they had lost their apartment. After this last disturbance the landlord told Allison's mother that they would have to move. They were two months behind in rent. He had given them notice before, but this time he meant it. Allison went with her mother and the other kids to the shelter, but she didn't even last the first night. They got into a screaming match over the restrictions Allison would have to observe in order for her to stay with the family in the unit. Security is a serious issue for the shelter, but nobody was going to tell Allison when she could come and go or who she could bring home if she felt like it. So Allison took her backpack and left the shelter. When she showed up at her aunt's place, her aunt had reluctantly taken her in. She said Allison could stay for the night, but she should get help from Social Services to find a place to stay, because that's what they were there for. What her aunt meant, but did not say, was that she was afraid of Allison's father, drunk or sober, and she knew Allison was no angel either. She didn't want anything to do with either of them, and there was no way she was going to let Allison stay after breakfast in the morning.

Vicky had seen Allison on her way up to the principal's office, and Marty told anyone who wanted to listen that Allison was out on the street with no one to take her in. Vicky knew that their church often helped families in crisis and that they had a connection of some kind with a family shelter. She called her mother and told her about Allison's problem. Her mother agreed that it sounded like a case the outreach worker at their church would probably be able to do something about and said she would call her immediately. So Vicky met Allison outside the principal's office to tell her that she thought their church could offer her some help in finding a place to live temporarily, and Allison seemed very grateful.

Allison and Marty went for burgers at a fast-food place near the school. Allison's imitation of Vicky rushing to rescue her from sleeping on the street sent them both into a fit of giggling. She could stay with her current boyfriend, but he was always broke, so she would have to get some money from somewhere. Allison would tell the church worker she was going to stay with her aunt, but that she needed money for clothes and emergency stuff, and the worker would probably come across with something; so, it would work out. That was one bit of gossip Allison knew Marty would not share with the whole school. Nobody would ever find out how she had used Vicky.

To Vicky, calling Allison seemed a logical choice, although Vicky's decision to go to her was anything but logical. She was sick with the worry that she was pregnant and needed to talk to someone, so she called Marty looking for Allison's phone number and was relieved to find Allison was there with her. She unburdened herself in one great flood of tears. She had to find out for sure, she said, if she was pregnant, and she needed to talk to somebody.

"Pregnant? Gee, Vicky I don't know. That's not good. I'm just so shocked that it happened to you." Allison covered the phone and grinned at Marty.

Marty was at her elbow and she doubled over giggling as Vicky talked, which was making it hard for Allison to keep the giggle out of her own voice.

"Well, if you want to know for sure, it's easy. They have these kits at all the drugstores, you know, and you can test yourself at home. You don't need a prescription or anything. They're out on the shelves and you can just pick one up. Like, my mom told me all about them and I read the instructions on her kit. Before we split up, you know, and she went to stay in the shelter." Marty poked her in the back and the two of them rolled onto the bed, with Allison trying to cover the mouthpiece so Vicky wouldn't hear them laughing.

"A kit?" Vicky said. "And then you use it to measure the results against a chart or something like that? Suppose you read the results wrong, or made a mistake or something. I don't know, Allison."

Allison finally lost it, and Marty had to take the phone, although she was giggling too, but Vicky didn't seem to notice.

"Hi Vicky. It's Marty. I heard what you were telling Allison. Look, this is really easy. I mean, you can't screw up the test." Allison bit her knuckle to stifle her laugh and Marty snorted, realizing the expression she had used. She held the phone against her arm to muffle the noise, and when she could talk again she said, "Sorry Vicky, Mom called me and I didn't want to talk when she was in the room. Just hold on for a minute."

Allison was staying at Marty's place because her boyfriend, her current boyfriend, had kicked her out. That was a major inconvenience, but at the moment the two of them were hysterical over Vicky's call, and Allison's problem could wait for a while. Vicky was so naive that she would never have believed that they were laughing at her, but then, she would never have guessed that Marty had already had an abortion or that pregnancy was more of an inconvenience than any sort of moral or ethical crisis for either of them. But the one thing Vicky did know as a result of this conversation was that if her life was to be turned upside down by finding out that she was pregnant, she wanted to hear it from a doctor. She wanted absolute certainty, and the findings from some do-it-yourself home kit just wouldn't do it. She had been to a walk-in medical clinic not far from the school when she'd cut her hand and needed to get a few stitches to close the cut. She would go there tomorrow, see a doctor she did not know and get the answer she needed immediately.

Her relationship with Steve changed as soon as she began to suspect she was pregnant. Suddenly, everything was wrong. There's nothing natural about getting pregnant at sixteen. There was no point to holding hands or just hanging out when you wanted to scream because your world was suddenly closing in on you. What was the point of worrying about homework or tests or how your hair looks when you were losing control of your own body? It wasn't hers anymore. Soon it would be on a schedule of its own. She felt disconnected and alone. It was as though she was becoming a different person and she didn't know herself anymore. Everything was strange and scary and she knew nothing would ever be the same again.

She couldn't go to her own doctor. He was their family doctor, and she had known him since she was a baby. It would be just as hard to face him as it was to face her own father. So Vicky signed out of class on Friday morning and went to the walk-in clinic. The nurse asked her what her problem was and she said she had constipation and stomach cramps and wanted to have it checked out. She asked to see a female doctor, and the nurse said Dr. DeAngelo would be in to see her when she was free. She hadn't told Steve that she thought she was pregnant and she just couldn't ask him to come to the clinic with her. So, now she was alone in the examination room and she was afraid of what the result of the examination would prove.

Dr. DeAngelo was very professional and after a complete examination she confirmed Vicky's suspicions. She was near the end of her first trimester and, from all appearances, she could expect to deliver in late June. When the doctor asked if Vicky wanted her to call her parents, Vicky shook her head. The doctor nodded. She tried to talk to Vicky about her situation and what preparations she needed to make for the baby's arrival, but Vicky started crying and shook her head. Dr. DeAngelo had seen it all before. This girl needed help, but if she wasn't ready to accept it there was nothing anyone could do. Even at sixteen, Vicky had the legal right to say how she wanted to be treated. She was obviously scared sick by the whole thing, but she was also a walk-in patient Dr. DeAngelo did not know, one she would probably never see again. And medically, nothing more was required at present. All she could do was advise Vicky to contact her own family doctor as soon as possible and see someone she could talk to about her situation. Dr. DeAngelo knew a woman at Social Services who did family counselling and would be a good person to help Vicky work through all her options. She wished Vicky well, left the examination room and stopped to ask the receptionist to dig out the social worker's business card for her. But by the time the receptionist had found it, Vicky was already walking to the bus stop.

It was a little before 11:00 when Vicky arrived back at school. Classes changed at 11:00, and she was closing her locker when she saw Steve coming down the hall toward her. He was in the middle of a group of three or four losers from their next class. Not guys he usually hung around with, just jerks who'd attached themselves to him for a laugh and wouldn't go away, but Vicky couldn't know that. They were laughing and horsing around as they came down the hall, and Steve was acutely embarrassed by their stupid antics. When the guys saw her, they became louder and they seemed to grow in size as they came nearer.

She turned to avoid them and move away, but a knot of girls from her next class were standing together behind her, blocking her way. They would not move to let her by, and as she forced her way through them, the malicious giggling started as she passed.

They knew! They all knew! Vicky felt everyone gawking at her. Suddenly she couldn’t breathe. She had no thought of where she would go or what she would do, but she had to get out of school and away from everyone.

She fled to the food court at the mall. No one would notice her there, and she could sit at a plastic table for as long as she wanted to, or until the canned Christmas music drove her out. It was Friday, December 22. School was finished for the Christmas holidays, so she wouldn’t have to deal with the kids at school for the next two weeks. She felt relieved that she had a little time to work things out, although she was not sure what she meant by “work things out,” nor how much better she really did feel. Vicky was becoming accustomed to the terrible confusion inside. She couldn’t remember what normal felt like anymore.

The cleaner came by and scowled at her as she dumped the pile of damp serviettes from the ashtray into the garbage. Vicky looked up absently, saw the clock, and a new wave of panic swept over her. It was 2:00 p.m. She had been sitting in the food court since a little after 11:00 that morning, and all she had worked out so far was that with Christmas holidays starting today, she would not have to see the kids at school for the next two weeks. What about the rest of her life? How was she going to tell her parents? How could she have a baby at sixteen? And what about Steve? She had not thought of him for hours, and as she remembered him and the jerks who were with him, a new wave of loathing and confusion swept over her.

She went home. What else was there to do? Her mother was home early from the office and called out “Hi” to her. Wonderful smells emanated from the kitchen, but she registered them mechanically, as she might recognize the smell of fresh paint. Vicky washed her face and changed into her work clothes. She worked part-time at a florist shop, and because it was

Christmas, she would be busy until 10:00 tonight and all day Saturday. Even Sunday would be a working day.

She avoided conversation as much as she could, and her mother, still busy in the kitchen, didn't seem to notice. Her father came home from his exercise class at the hospital just as she was leaving early for work. They said "Hi" in passing, and he, too, was apparently unaware of her emotional state, although she was sure it was written all over her face.

Work went well. She sailed through the orders, one after another. Check the type and number of flowers. Make up the arrangements. Set out the potted plants. Wrap and address each order, then set it out, ready for Chuck as soon as he got back from the last delivery. So many cards, so many dollars in the till, so many hours until morning, then do it all over again. That was easy. Nothing to it. Just run on automatic.

Saturday morning came and went, and nothing unusual happened, but about 3:00 in the afternoon, Greg, the manager, usually so quiet and easygoing, called her into the workroom and started yelling at her. He was stressed out and she had never seen him so upset before. He kept flipping through the order forms he was holding, then pointed at her with them.

"Vicky, what's wrong with you today? Three customers sent orders back because they were all wrong. It was stuff they hadn't ordered and wouldn't accept. That's close to eighty bucks down the drain and an hour of Chuck's time wasted. I can't afford screw-ups like this." Her shoulders slumped, and he stood looking at her, waiting for a reply. But Vicky didn't reply. She just started crying, grabbed her coat from behind the door and ran from the store.

It took an hour on the bus to get home and it was almost dark as she walked into the house. She was home too early, even for a normal Saturday, and her mother knew something was wrong immediately. Her father was reading in the living room and called out to her as she passed, "Hi dear. You're home early. Anything the matter? Vicky?"

Vicky paused to look at her father, tried to speak, but burst into tears instead and ran up to her room. He turned to his wife for a reaction, but she seemed as confused as he was. The only thing Donna Penrose knew for sure was that David must not get upset; she moved to calm him down immediately. Since the heart attack he had been unusually emotional and easily upset. The doctor had warned her that might happen. But he must not get excited. She worried because he would go on for hours stewing about trivial things and sending his blood pressure soaring.

"Now what do you suppose is bothering her?" David said, folding his paper and leaning forward in his chair. "She looks all upset. I think you should go talk to her. Find out what's bothering her."

Donna was beside him now and making soothing noises, almost as if he were a child in need of comfort, and he hated that.

"Donna, stop that!" David slapped the paper down on the coffee table, turned to face her and took her hands in his. "I had a heart attack, Donna. I didn't go simple all of a sudden," he said, softening his tone considerably. "Now, please, quit fussing over me and go see what's up with Vicky."

"Oh, I think I know what it's all about," she said. "Steve didn't come over on Friday, and he's called several times today but wouldn't leave a message. He just says he'll call her back later. They've had a spat or something, I expect. It's probably nothing to worry about. And certainly nothing you need to get all worked up about."

"There you go again, telling me not to worry, like I was a six-year-old. I'll look after my blood pressure; you go talk to Vicky and see what's bothering her. Steve would have known she was working today, and he wouldn't have called today unless he expected her to be home. Now, that doesn't make any sense. So, please, go and talk to her. I think it's important. She looked very upset."

Donna could almost see his blood pressure rising. This wasn't good for him. She would have to go and try to talk to her, but if Vicky had wanted to talk she would have come down and said so. She went up and tapped on her door, but Vicky didn't even open it. She just called out that she was tired and was going to bed early and asked her mother not to worry about her.

But Vicky wasn't just tired. She was exhausted. She wanted to stop the film playing in her head, but she couldn't turn it off. She walked the halls of the school over and over again. There were the girls from her class, standing behind her, quiet and malicious, until she turned to leave, and then blocking her way and giggling at her humiliation. And Steve looking so embarrassed when he saw her. And the crude jerks who were with him, laughing so loud and joking about her. She could see herself sitting in the food court at the mall crying for hours, feeling trapped and alone and knowing there was no way to escape what was happening. That was the last fuzzy thought she had as she drifted off to sleep, and it would be the first conscious thought she had when she awoke in the morning. There was no way out.

Vicky dressed quietly Sunday morning, intending to go into work. She didn't know what else to do. But when she checked the time and realized that she had slept past noon, she knew that something was dreadfully wrong. She was losing touch. She needed time to get away, to think things out, but if you are alone and in your own bed and time slips away from you, where do you go to be even more alone? And what good would more thinking do when nothing could change the facts?

She started down the stairs, a sense of panic already rising in her. If she could just get to work she would be all right. She could drop into the routine and make it through the day, and everything would be all right. She didn't make it to the front door. Her mother was sitting on the couch, her father was standing before the picture window, and Steve was perched on the chair opposite the television, looking very uncomfortable. They turned to her in unison and just looked at her, startled by her sudden appearance. She gasped and, in that one humiliating instant, she realized that they also knew. Everybody knew. Everybody was talking about her. They were all just gawking at her.

She recovered quickly enough to grab her coat from the chair where she had thrown it last night and was out the door and down the steps in a second. She was sobbing openly now as she reached the sidewalk. They reacted too slowly to catch her as she left the house, and the bus was standing at the stop as she reached the curb. Vicky boarded, and they lost the bus from view as it lumbered away down the street.

David Penrose came out onto the porch to put his arm around his wife and bring her back inside. It was cold and Vicky was out of sight now. Steve was still standing by the front window, staring down the street after the bus, as they came in. They sat in silence for awhile. It was an "if only" moment, one of those moments you wish you could relive because you know something important has happened in that moment and you messed up somehow. And if it turns out badly, you know you will relive that moment for the rest of your life.

"It's all my fault," Steve said. "I'm so sorry. I'm just so, so terribly sorry."

Donna made coffee, although no one really wanted any. She set out the pot and cups and they all came and sat around the kitchen table. She poured coffee into three cups, but no one reached for them.

"Well, Steve," David said, "let's be clear about it. Are you trying to say that Vicky is pregnant? Is that it?"

Steve nodded and lowered his head. He looked as if he'd been whipped, and given the shame he was feeling, that was not too surprising. "I think so. I mean, I only heard about it from kids at school. They were all talking about it on Friday. She must have known for weeks, but she never said a word to me about it. She started acting strange about a week ago and that's when she must have decided to find out. Then she didn't want to see me and she wouldn't talk to me. But she called Allison Myers to find out how you get tested to see if you're pregnant, and that's how the story got out. Allison and Marty were giggling themselves sick and telling everybody how dumb they thought she was.

"We didn't plan it. We didn't talk about it or mean to do it. It just sort of happened. It's so stupid. I mean, we knew better. If we were going to fool around, we would have taken precautions, but we never intended to do anything, so...and now she's pregnant."

Donna poured some cream into one of the cups, stirring in sugar, more for something to do than because she really wanted the coffee. "Well," she said, "I should have seen something was wrong long before this. There were plenty of signs that something was bothering her. She hasn't been sleeping well lately. She was distracted and not eating much, either. But then, she'd had this breakup, or fight, or whatever with you, and I just assumed that was the problem. Was that the problem? Did you have a breakup over the pregnancy?"

"No, honestly, Mrs. Penrose. We never talked about it and I haven't talked to her since I heard the rumours at school. I don't know how I would have reacted if she had told me, but we wouldn't have quarrelled. We just wouldn't. We love each other. That's not going to change, whether she's pregnant or not."

"And you weren't going to have sex either, were you?" David shook his head and looked at Steve. "You're only sixteen and so is she, and you think you are in love. How do you know what you'll feel in six months or a year? And it isn't just you two anymore. There's the baby now and you two hadn't figured that into the mix either, and you still haven't. So don't tell me about loving her just like nothing's changed, because it has. Everything has changed and...and...."

His face grew pale. He struggled to breathe and slowly began to slump forward onto the table.

"David!" Donna was up in a flash and lowering him to the floor. "Call 911," she screamed, and Steve lunged for the wall phone and punched in the number immediately.

"Oh, God! It's all my fault! Oh, God!" With the call completed, Steve had time to babble and dither, until Donna called him to help her drag the table and chairs out of the way. They heard the siren and knew the ambulance would be there any minute. They laid David out on the floor, and he began to breathe more easily, able to talk to them in short, little gasps. Donna was still kneeling beside David, telling him to lie still and breathe slowly, even as paramedics strode into the kitchen and took charge of their patient.

They followed as he was carried out of the house, and Donna climbed into the ambulance to be with him for the ride to the hospital. She called to Steve and told him to wait at the house in case Vicky came home. She would call when she knew how David was doing. Steve went back into the house and surveyed the broken coffee pot and the mess of coffee and stuff that had been knocked to the floor. There would be plenty of time for him to clean up the mess in the kitchen while he waited to hear how Mr. Penrose was and for Vicky to come home.

But Vicky wasn't planning to come home. How long she rode the bus or where she was exactly, she couldn't tell. It stopped and she got off. She walked. She sat down on a bench for a while, then she began walking again. It was getting dark now, and she was still walking. The sounds of Christmas faded behind her. The tasteless songs, the oily good wishes for a happy holiday, the endless repetitions of "White Christmas"—all of it was finally behind her.

Somehow, the thought that tomorrow was Christmas hadn't occurred to her during this whole ordeal, and when it did she found she didn't care. It was cold, and she didn't care about that either. She was numb inside and grateful for that dreadful inner stillness. She didn't feel bitterness toward Allison or Marty. She didn't feel anything, and even the humiliation at school didn't matter any more. It was over. She just didn't care. And that's how she came to be sitting alone on a park bench overlooking the river on this Christmas Eve, drifting from despair into nothingness.

She looked around and saw the fence and, a few feet beyond, the slow, patient river. She knew where she was now. This was Riverside Park, close to the Denton City Parkway. She had come here many times with her family for picnics or just to walk by the river. That must be why she was here now, to lean on the rail and gaze at the river, the quiet, gentle, deep river. So close. So peaceful. She had only to lean over the rail a little more and it would be all over in a minute. No baby, no school, no one to laugh at her anymore. She closed her eyes and drifted. The rail was cold and smooth beneath her hands. The noise of the water was soothing. She could join the river.

Suddenly, she stiffened and gripped the rail. There was something in the water just below the surface, floating with the current. It had no right to be in the river, not now. She looked closer and saw it was nothing, a plastic shopping bag with a happy face, just below the surface but undulating in the water, the big, silly face grinning up at her. With a jolt she remembered the pile of garbage bags she'd helped to fill at the river cleanup back in the spring. Mounds of plastic trash, cans, bottles, tires, condoms, discarded clothing and all manner of filthy, stinking stuff dragged up from the river and piled on the shore. She shuddered, imagining herself floating amid all that muck, and a wave of revulsion swept over her. She turned from the river and sat down heavily on the bench again. She was very cold. She could barely feel her fingers. She was in a little pool of dim light, and all around was dark and quiet and threatening. The enormity of what she had almost done settled in on her and with it came an irrational panic, a desire to scream and run from this place.

She knew which way to go to get back to the road, but she hesitated. She didn't want to leave her little pool of light and walk into the dark. The road seemed so far away. She stumbled up and started in that direction, but turned to look back at the light, tempted to return to her bench, even as she had been tempted by the river. She forced herself into the darkness and hurried stiffly toward the road. She could just make out a glimmer of light in the distance. She hurried toward it, unable to see the path in the dark and terrified she might trip and fall, and freeze here, alone, in this terrible place.

She ran, shaking with the cold, until she burst into the blessed light of the street lamp at the edge of the road. But the only sound she heard on that normally busy highway was the sound of her own breathing. There were no cars, no buses, no trucks. It was Christmas Eve, and it seemed no one was on the road on this cold, dark night. She was at a bus stop with a bench inside an open glass shelter, under the glare of harsh, cold light. She sank down and wept. She was too tired to run further, and apart from this one bright, empty shelter, the darkness was empty all around her.

She could see he was big, but like a shadow in the pale glow from the flashing red and blue of the car lights. He did not approach, but called to her from a few feet away.

"Miss? Are you all right? Miss, can you hear me? Are you all right?"

A second voice answered, "She probably can't hear you. She looks like she's right out of it. What do you want to do? Get her up and moving or call it in and let the emergency techs take her in?"

"Well, let's take a closer look first. Most of their units were out on call a while ago. She could freeze by the time they get here. Be careful, though. If she's too far gone, she may turn on you."

"What, you think she may have a knife or something?"

"I've told you before: they can be dangerous, even if they aren't armed. They may scratch or bite, or even just spit on you, and she could have anything from TB to AIDS. So, grip her tight and don't let her twist away from you suddenly."

They came at her quickly, one on each side, and took a firm grip on her arms, one hand on the wrist and one hand above the elbow on each side. They got her up and walked her to the car. One opened the door, the smaller one, she thought, not releasing her wrist, and they eased her into the back seat. They had quickly patted down her coat and over her pants' pockets, but she would not remember that.

"Shall I call it in?"

"She seems to be coming 'round. Let's just give her a few minutes to warm up in the car and see what happens. Do you notice anything odd about her?"

"Like what?"

"Well, now that you can see her in the light, what's your assessment of her?"

"Oh. I see what you mean. Well, she doesn't stink. No smell of alcohol or excessive body odour. She hasn't puked on herself, or messed herself, so far as I can see. She appears clean and shows no obvious abrasions or wounds. She's dressed normally and looks to me like any ordinary teenager."

"That would be my guess too. And it looks like she is about to join us."

"Miss, are you all right? You're in a patrol car, and we are city police officers. Can you hear me? Do you understand what I am saying to you? Can you tell us who you are?"

They came into focus slowly. One was older and bigger and one was much smaller and seemed much younger. And then she saw it was a female police officer.

"My name is Vicky Penrose. I'm in high school and I live on Benson Road—146 Benson Road. I don't know what else...."

"I'd say you were doing fine, and welcome back, Vicky. For a moment there we weren't sure if you were going to come back to us or not. I think you were about as close to being a Popsicle as anyone I have ever seen. We're going to run you up to the hospital, just because you were so far out of it, and let the medical people look at you." The female officer was already driving and the male officer had pulled out a notebook and was jotting something down in it.

"Do you want to tell me how you came to be sitting in the bus shelter at this time of night, Vicky? This is a very lonely stretch of the park system and there is nobody and nothing around for several kilometers in either direction, so how did you get here and what were you doing here all alone?"

"I took the bus earlier this afternoon." She paused and seemed confused. "And I walked through the park and I sat on a bench in the park by the river." She paused again and began shivering violently. "And it got dark so fast. So I followed the path out to the road, but there was no bus and there was nothing to do but wait in the shelter. And then you came."

He made a note and seemed to consider it for a moment. "Okay," he said. "Now that you are fully awake, will you let the doctors have a look at you, just to make sure you haven't suffered any ill effects from your exposure? You don't have to, and we won't try to force you, but it would be foolish to leave the hospital before someone looks at you. Is that okay with you?"

"Yes, but I think I'm just cold and tired. And hungry. I'm very hungry. I haven't thanked you both for helping me, have I? I was really in trouble there, wasn't I?"

"Yes, you were. I think another hour or so and you wouldn't be here now. Hypothermia is far more serious and more common than most people realize, and you were pretty far gone. Hopefully you don't have any frostbite, nothing serious, anyway. You were very lucky."

At the hospital, the female officer—Katherine McCartal—brought her a coffee and put lots of sugar in it. She stayed while Vicky registered and waited until she was called into the examination room. She asked if Vicky would like her to call anyone, her parents or a boyfriend or anyone, but Vicky said she would call home herself as soon as the examination was finished. She checked to see that Vicky had money for a cab home and took a quick peek at her identification when she filled out the forms.

Officer McCartal stood to go, but turned to Vicky before she left and said quietly, "Are you going to try it again or was once enough?"

Vicky's eyes widened and then she looked down. "I think I'll just go home and get some sleep. Things always seem better in the daylight. Thank you again. I'll go home when I leave here. I'll never do anything...." Her voice trailed off and she looked away.

The young policewoman looked hard at her for a moment, obviously wondering whether to say anything more or not. Finally she said, "Well, this is only my second month with the police force, so I don't have a whole lot of experience. Jeff says there's no need to push it, so you can do what you like, but I think you need to talk to someone. What is it, anyway? Boyfriend trouble? School? Family? Pregnant? Oh."

The officer had read it in her face, and Vicky was crying again. "All of it I guess. It all just came on so fast and everything fell apart. I was ashamed to tell them, my parents, I mean, but they know now, so I just have to get on with it, don't I? But it's like I have to start life all over again and nothing's like it used to be. I'm not making any sense, am I? It scares me, to think about it, I mean. I'll never do anything like this again. You were both very kind. Thank you again. My mother doesn't have to know I was picked up by the police, does she? Like, you didn't arrest me or anything, did you, and nobody from the police will call, will they?"

Officer McCartal shook her head. "You were given a lift because you were stranded at a bus stop after the buses had stopped running. It's no big deal. The only thing that might get sticky is trying to explain to your parents why you got stranded at the bus stop in the first place. It sounds like you've got a lot of things to talk over with your parents anyway, so it might be smart to put it all out on the table and get it over with. But that's up to you. Hope it all works out for you."

She waved and was gone. In a few minutes Vicky was called into the examination room. She was seen by a doctor, who assured her she was fine and told her she could go home. Now all she had to do was screw up her courage to phone and explain where she had been from lunchtime until nearly 11:00 p.m. She had a sandwich from a machine and a soft drink, worked up her resolve and called. She was thrown off balance when Steve answered, unsure for a moment if she had punched in his number by mistake.

"Steve? You're still at our house? Is Mom still up? I have to talk to her."

"Vicky! It's been hours since you left. We were all sick worrying about you. Are you okay? Where are you?"

"I'm at the hospital—Eastside General. I'm okay. It's a long story, but I'm just using the pay phone here. I don't want to talk just now, Steve. I'm glad you're there. Call Mom for me, Steve. I have to talk to her."

"Vicky, that's the problem. I can't call your mom because she is at the hospital right now. Did you say Eastside General? Because that's where she is with your dad right now. After you left, well actually right after you left we all..."

"Daddy's in the hospital again? Right here at Eastside General? How is he? No, never mind. I'll have to find them. The reception desk will know where they are. I have to go. I should have known. Oh Steve, what if it's really bad this time? It's all my fault. I have to go."

"Vicky, no. Wait a minute. Your dad's going to be okay. Your mom called me a while ago to see if you were home yet. It was another heart attack, but a very mild one, and he was in hospital minutes after it started. He's going to be okay."

"I don't understand. Why did she call you and why are you still at our house?"

The long hours Steve sat waiting for Vicky to come home and the frustration he felt at being unable to do anything finally bubbled over in resentment and he spoke more sharply than he had intended. "I'm at your house because I've been here since you ran out this morning. And I am still here because your mom and dad are worried sick about you. Your dad had another attack about lunchtime, when we were all talking, and when your mom went with your dad in the ambulance she asked me to stay and wait in case you came home. Then she phoned to ask if you were home yet, and that's when she told me that your dad was going to be okay. And I'm still here because I love you, and you didn't want to talk to me about the baby, and we need to talk. So, okay. Go find your mom, and when you come home we can talk. All right? I need to see you, Vicky, and there's the baby and, like, stuff we need to talk about."

"Not tonight, Steve." Vicky couldn't take it all in, but she had to find her mom before she did anything else. "It's late now and

I'm really tired. It'll be way into the morning before I get home. Go home now. We can get together tomorrow or something, but I have to go, okay? Bye."

She hung up and hurried back to the reception desk to ask about her father. He was all she could think about and she needed to be sure he was really all right. She followed the directions to his room and peeked in. Her father was asleep, with the typical bedside tray holding a glass of water on one side; there was an intravenous drip into his arm on the other. Her mother looked up and smiled tiredly as Vicky tiptoed into the room, and they fell into an embrace, holding each other. Vicky began to sob and Donna gripped her arm and guided her quickly out of the room and down the hall to a quiet waiting area. Off to the side was a mini kitchen with a sink, a fridge and a kettle. Donna put the kettle on to make tea for both of them. She was methodical and slow, thinking through the fact that her daughter had suddenly shown up after twelve hours without a word from her. Vicky took the tea, neither of them speaking for a few minutes, both of them aware of the tension between them.

"Tell me about Dad. Is he really going to be all right? I spoke to Steve and he said you called earlier and said he was fine, but is he really?"

Donna smiled tiredly. "You can't say he's fine. He came through the attack and he's out of danger, for now, at least."

Vicky held the cup in both hands, looking at her mother until she had to look away, and her gaze drifted down to the floor. Donna sipped her tea and put the cup down. She leaned back in her chair and breathed out a long, tired sigh.

"It's too early to say he is fine. Your father is sick with heart disease and high blood pressure. You know that. They can help him to build up his strength and they can help him to lower his blood pressure, but I don't think he will ever be the man he was. They can't make him new again."

Vicky studied her mother as she spoke. Donna looked as though she'd aged ten years since yesterday. She was grey and haggard. Her hair was limp and untidy. She seemed to have lost weight, but maybe she had been losing weight for some time and Vicky just hadn't noticed. Donna finished her tea, collected both cups and put them by the sink. Then she turned to look at Vicky.

"I've been worried sick about you. Where have you been and what have you been doing for the last twelve hours? Your father asked hours ago if you were home. You have to be here when he wakes up again. So tell me what happened."

She had no answer to give to her mother. The truth was that she had come close to ending her own life in that filthy river, only to come even closer to losing it by accident in the cold, and it was all so stupid. She looked up at her mother, too ashamed to tell her, but there was no sign of softening in her mother's face. She put her face in her hands and started to cry again.

Donna stood, impassive, patient. Finally, she came to stand beside Vicky, put her arms around her and pulled her close. She kissed the top of her head, and Vicky rested in her arms and felt their comfort.

"You've cried enough, Vicky," Donna said, almost in a whisper, her tone flat, as if all the emotion had been drained out of her a long time ago. "You must answer me now. Where have you been and what have you been doing for the last twelve hours?"

"I can't tell you. It's too stupid and too horrible." Vicky clung to her mother until Donna pushed her away.

Donna took Vicky's face in both of her hands and held her at arm's length so she could look into her face. "You're not a little girl any more, Vicky," she said forcefully. "You have obligations and responsibilities and one of them is to your father. In a few minutes we are going back into his room, and if he is awake, the first thing he will want to know is where you have been and why you didn't call home for twelve hours while the doctors here were working to keep his heart going. And you are going to tell him something reasonable, because if you go in there and you weep and moan like an orphan sheep, you may very well kill him. Do you understand me?"

Donna spoke with a sharpness that shocked her, and Vicky started crying again. But she stopped abruptly. She swallowed hard and took in a big breath, reaching out for her mother again.

"Tell me everything." Holding her, Donna said quietly, "Every last detail. And then we'll come up with something to tell your father, and we will keep it as close to the truth as possible. Now tell me all of it."

Vicky started and stopped several times, wanting to gloss over whole segments of the story, but her mother was relentless in her questioning and perceptive in her insights. It took about a half-hour to finish the story, and Donna didn't flinch at the account of Vicky's flirtation with the river or her fortunate discovery by the police at the bus stop. Donna sat back down in her chair. She took in a sharp breath and let it out slowly, gathering herself to deal with the story.

"Well," she said, "the bus ride going on for hours is plausible and it's true. Stress that when you talk to him. Now we need to account for the time you spent in the park."

"I came in from the far side just as it was getting dark and I walked to the lookout. I really didn't think about how far it was from the bus stop. But it's a really long way."

"Yes," Donna said, nodding absently. "And you were feeling sorry for yourself and you found the bench we used to stop at and you just sat and daydreamed about the picnics we used to take there. And you were feeling ashamed about getting pregnant and you just sat crying for a long time. That makes sense." She was talking quietly, more to herself than to Vicky.

"It's true. I was ashamed about letting you both down," Vicky added quietly, her gaze returning to the floor. "That's what I was thinking about for most of the time—how I had let you down. I'm so sorry, Mom. I really am."

"Yes, well. But we need to account for more hours. It would be about 8:00 p.m. by now, in this reconstruction of your story, so what did you do from then until you showed up here at 11:00?"

"I can tell him about the bus stop. That's true. I can even tell him about the police coming and finding me and thinking I needed help. And I did, because the buses weren't running and there was no phone or a gas station or anywhere I could call for help."

Donna nodded. "All right, that makes sense." She got up and emptied the last of the tea from their cups into the sink. She dropped the plastic inserts into the garbage and put the cup parts back on the shelf. "And then they brought you here. You saw the doctor just to make sure you were all right, and then you found out we were here. And you and I just talked while your father slept." She turned back to Vicky, thinking. "What did we talk about? Something about when you were a little girl, I think. Something about how much you loved being with him somewhere. Can you think about anything you did together that he would remember?"

"Shopping," Vicky said immediately. "I loved it when he took me grocery shopping and I had him all to myself, and he would spoil me with toys or something silly or take me with him to the coffee shop and I would get a drink too."

"Really? You liked going shopping with him? I didn't know that." And after a moment she added, "Well, there, now we really did have a chat and some tea and a little rest, and that did take up some time, and now you have your story if he asks about it."

Vicky started to say again how sorry she was, but Donna told her that what was done, was done. What mattered now, she said, and all that mattered right now, was how well they shielded her father from the upsetting details of her ordeal. And Vicky knew she was right.

David awoke about midnight, and Vicky was there to talk to him, but he was just pleased to have her there. He didn't even ask where she had been or what she had been doing. He would eventually, of course, but for now he was satisfied just to have her kiss him good night and let him go back to sleep. As he was drifting off he insisted they go home and get some sleep, themselves. He was fine, he said, and they could come tomorrow afternoon, unless the doctors discharged him and sent him home before that.

They rode in silence in the taxi on the way home, until Donna told Vicky what Steve had told them about her ordeal at school. Finally she said, "You have to give Steve credit, you know. There was no way to keep the story quiet once it was common gossip at school, and we would have heard about it eventually. But coming over to tell us about it first-hand and taking responsibility himself for the baby; well, that took courage. And he said he didn't understand why you didn't tell him about the baby yourself. He only found out about it from the kids at school on Friday; and he had a rough time at school, too." Donna didn't say anything else and Vicky was grateful because she needed time to absorb what she had just been told. She was still mulling it over as they entered the house.

Vicky stopped at the foot of the stairs and looked up at her mother. It was late and they were very tired, but something needed to be said and they both knew it. "Mom, can I ask you something?" Donna stopped and waited for her to continue.

"I was afraid to tell you I was pregnant. I was ashamed to face you and Dad and I still am. And I told you about the park and the river and I think I might really have done it. It was so stupid, but I think I might have. And I just don't understand."

"What don't you understand, Vicky? Were you expecting me to be shocked and to cry and carry on about how disappointed we are in you, is that it? And you tell me that I almost lost my daughter tonight." She paused, catching her breath. "And I don't react to that either. Is that what you don't understand?" Donna looked at her steadily, apparently calm, her head bent slightly forward, the only sign of the stress she was under.

Vicky nodded, but said nothing.

"When you rushed out of the house this morning I was terribly upset, because I was afraid you might do something foolish, but then I had your father to worry about and I was with him for hours at the hospital and I didn't know if he'd even survive. I didn't have much time to think about you then. But once you came into his room at the hospital, I already had you back, didn't I? Safe and well, and what might have happened doesn't really matter anymore, does it? At least it doesn't matter right now."

Vicky said nothing. She picked up her coat from the chair where she had dropped it when they came in. Donna stood on the stair, waiting for Vicky to look up at her again before going on.

"And it's the same with the baby. Getting pregnant at your age, and with your father so sick; I just can't cope with it now." Donna put out her hand to the banister to steady herself. "Let's talk about it tomorrow." She turned to climb the stairs, but stopped and stood for another moment as if unsure she had the strength to finish her thought. When she spoke again there were tears in her eyes. "I don't know what you're going to do about the baby, but I'll tell you this. I think you're going to ache for that baby for the rest of your life."

Vicky came to her quickly and held her, and her cheek was wet with her mother's tears. For the first time she understood the weight of the responsibility she had undertaken and a little of the impact she was having on all of their lives.

Vicky called Steve sometime around 2:00 that morning. She had to talk to him. He was awake, or woke quickly enough to get the phone on the second ring. They talked for hours, until they couldn't stay awake any longer. Steve asked Vicky where she'd been when she was gone for so long, and she told him everything, just as she had told it to her mother. She apologized for thinking Steve was ashamed of her at school, because he had done the right thing to come and explain about the baby to her parents, and he wouldn't have done that if he was ashamed of her. She was proud of him for that. They talked about everything. They talked about nothing. Sometimes they stopped talking altogether and just listened to the quiet. Steve loved her and wanted to marry her. She knew that, but they would have to wait until they were older, and Steve knew that, too, and that was okay. They were quiet for a long time, until Vicky said that she knew she wouldn't be able to keep the baby and raise it herself at home with her parents. She hadn't asked her mother and she wouldn't, because her dad was so sick. It just wouldn't work. Steve asked if she knew what she was going to do about the baby, and she said she really didn't know right now. But they had lots of time before it was born.

The last thing she said before she fell asleep was to ask him if he would come over for breakfast in the morning, and he said sure, just like that. She said good night, fumbled the phone to its cradle and was asleep before she let go of it. But Steve was wide awake now. What would they do about the baby?

Steve parked his dad's car out in front of the house and stood, shifting from one foot to the other at the kitchen door, suddenly shy in Donna's presence. Vicky brought him in to sit at the kitchen table and the tension eased as they ate breakfast. Donna said she was going back to the hospital and asked if Steve would bring Vicky over to stay with her dad in the afternoon. He nodded, and shortly after breakfast Donna left for the hospital.

Alone together for the first time in several weeks, everything was awkward and strange between them. Breakfast had been fine. It was as if the past week hadn't happened, and even Donna had seemed relaxed and remarkably cheerful. But now, alone, they were hesitant, uncertain of each other.

Vicky put the kettle back on and got a plate of cookies out of the fridge. Steve said he was full, but when the tea was poured he managed to pack several of them away, because, he said, they hadn't had any Christmas stuff and they deserved them. Vicky giggled and said she was eating for two now and she was entitled to get goofy because she was pregnant. They held hands and sat at the table and giggled for a minute. But the giggling stopped and they sat looking away from each other, knowing they still had things they needed to talk about.

"When you were thinking about the river," Steve asked, "did you think about the baby, you know, like, if you died, he'd die too?" It was an abrupt question. She had told him about the river the night before, and the thought that she might actually have killed herself still disturbed him.

"It was strange, you know. I couldn't have an abortion. I just couldn't. When he's born he'll be so tiny and beautiful, with little hands and feet, and if we were married he would be our baby to keep, and how could you kill your own baby? I mean, killing a baby just because he or she is, I don't know, inconvenient or something. That's no reason to kill a baby. That wouldn't make any sense. But if I died? I don't know. I guess I figured he was still part of me and he would be dead like the rest of me." Vicky got up and put the cookies back in the fridge. She closed the door and stood with her back to him. After a minute she turned and said, "I don't think I even tried to figure out what I was doing. I just wanted the hurt to stop. Does that make any sense?"

"Yeah, I think so. Sort of anyhow," he said. There was a pause and then Steve asked, "Would you have an abortion if the baby was really deformed, like, too sick to live, even if it was born alive?"

"I don't know. Maybe. If the baby was really hopelessly sick, I guess. But this baby is fine. Why are you asking about abortions? You don't...you aren't thinking I should have an abortion are you? Because I won't. I just couldn't."

"No. You can't have an abortion. It's like you said. It's stupid to kill a baby just because it comes along when you don't want it to. But we never talked about how we felt about abortion, and I thought we should."

"Why? Why should we talk about abortion now?"

"Because if you had an abortion, all the problem about having the baby would be gone. I would hate it if you had an abortion, but not having an abortion means you're going to have a baby around the end of June."

"We know that. What are you getting at? I don't understand what you're saying."

"What I'm saying is that in June, when you have the baby, you know you can't keep it and live here. You said that last night, because it would be too hard for your mom to help you with the baby and look after your dad, too. And we can't get married and keep it ourselves. We know that too. So, what are you going to do with this new baby? Our baby? We haven't talked about that."

"Well." She paused, considering the question for the first time. "Well, we'll have to give it up for adoption, I guess. What else is there to do? We could find a nice couple who want to adopt and..." She stopped halfway through the sentence. Steve stood up and reached out for her, and she came to him, and he held her as the idea became a reality for her. Her baby. Someone taking her baby and loving it, and it would become their baby. She began to cry.

He held her for a long time, until her sobs subsided and his own tears stopped. He tucked her head under his chin and said, "I thought about it last night after we hung up. You have to give him away right after he's born. We have to give him away to make sure he or she has a happy life, because we can't give it to him. And we need to know now that's what we have to do, because it will be hard when he's born."

Steve went on talking quietly until he was too choked up to talk, but she hadn't heard him. She was remembering what her mother had said last night. She hadn't understood her then. It made sense now, and she was right. She would ache for this baby for the rest of her life.

~

A Tale of Two Heroes

She waited near the administrative offices, sitting at a bench just out of sight of the clerks inside. At 9:00 a.m. the clerk opened the office door, flicked the overhead lights on and moved back behind the reception counter. Karen Hartley waited for her breathing to slow and her heart to stop pounding. It was time.

She entered the public offices of the Denton City Zoo, passed the gift shop, crossed to the wicket labelled School Tour Registration and waited for the clerk to notice her.

"Excuse me," she said. "Is this the place where the teachers come to let you know they're here with their classes for a tour of the zoo?"

The clerk smiled. Her name tag read Agnes Cunningham.

"Yes," she said. "Are you a teacher? Do you have a tour booked for today?" She had already noted Karen's worn jeans, scruffy coat and hair that looked as if it had never seen a hairbrush, let alone a professional cut. Just another parent, Agnes thought, about to ask me to take care of some trivial problem for her kid that she was too sloppy to take care of herself.

"Who me?" Karen said, her eyes going wide. "Not hardly. No, um, but my boy's coming to the zoo today with his class and, see, I forgot to give him his lunch kit. I thought you could maybe give it to his teacher when she gets here with her class." She hovered hopefully, eyes wide in expectation.

The clerk smiled. "Well, we don't do that sort of thing here, but I guess we can help you." She reached into a drawer beside her, extracted a label and laid it on the counter. "This is the teachers' registration wicket, not the lost and found, but I'll see his teacher gets it. What's your son's name?"

"Gee, thanks." Karen said all big eyes and toothy grin. She placed the Spiderman lunch kit on the counter and pushed it forward toward Agnes. "It's Arty, Arthur Henderson, and he'd be real upset if he lost his lunch kit. It's his special thing, you know."

Mrs. Cunningham smiled absently and wrote the name on the top half of the label.

"School? Teacher's name?" When Karen didn't answer immediately, Agnes looked up at her.

Karen hesitated. Even though she had anticipated the question, she was unsettled by it. What if she named a school that had no tours coming to the zoo today!

"Well, see that's the problem. We only moved to the city on the weekend and Arty didn't start school until yesterday." She shrugged her shoulders in a 'what can I say' gesture. "Moving and all, you know, but anyway, I don't remember the name of the school and I never met his teacher yet. But I'd recognize the school in a minute if I heard it."

Karen's heart was pounding, and her mouth was dry. She smiled her most helpless smile and waited. Mrs. Cunningham nodded indulgently and, if the truth be told, a little condescendingly, as well. She picked up the roster of school tours for that morning.

"Well, we have Meadowvale Elementary: Mrs. Applebee, grade five, from 10:00 to 2:00 in the west parking lot; Assumption Separate School: Mrs. Strong, grade four, from 11:00 to 1:30, east parking lot; Maple Ridge Composite School: Mr. Keeler, grade three, from 10:00 to 2:00, west parking lot; or..."

Mrs. Cunningham turned from Karen and asked another clerk behind her, "Mr. Keeler, from Maple Ridge Composite. Why's that name familiar?"

They both laughed.

"He called again, you know, a few minutes ago. His bus driver hadn't arrived yet and he wanted us to know he might be a few minutes late. Every year, at least two calls per visit." They laughed again.

"Er, excuse me." Karen had all the information she needed now and she was running late.

The clerk looked back to her, still holding that day's roster of tour groups.

"I remember the school name now. It was the first one on the list. Meadowvale Elementary School. I should have remembered. He's in grade five, so that must be his class. What did you say the teacher's name was?"

"Mrs. Applebee." She put the roster back in the basket beside her window and wrote the name of the teacher, the grade and the school on the label. She attached the label to the lunch kit and placed it under the counter. She looked at Karen again and said dismissively, "Okay. I'll see she gets it."

Karen thanked her and left quickly. It was only 9:20. She stuffed her gloves into her pockets, but kept her coat on. She walked up to the cafeteria, got a coffee and took it to a window overlooking the loading zone. If what she'd learned from the clerk was correct, she'd have about thirty minutes to kill.

She was shaking. Something in the clerk's look had bothered her. There was no reason the clerk should be suspicious, but exposing herself like that was risky. The lunch kit was clean. She'd stuffed it with a deli cinnamon bun, an apple and a Coke, just in case anyone got curious and opened it. And she hadn't touched any of it without gloves on. She checked the wall clock: 9:45. She drew a big breath. About fifteen minutes to go.

She thought about the confusion she'd created for Mrs. Applebee. It couldn't be helped. When Mrs. Applebee, the grade five teacher from Meadowvale Elementary School, checked in at the desk, as every teacher in charge of a school tour always did, she would be presented with a lunch kit for a kid she had never heard of. She'd freak. She'd phone her principal in a panic and ask if there was some kid named Arthur Henderson standing around at the school who was supposed to be on her bus. They'd go nuts looking for a kid that didn't exist.

At 9:55, the bus with "Maple Ridge" on a cardboard sign in the holder on the passenger side front window pulled up to the loading zone. A male teacher got out and herded the kids towards the reception area. That had to be Keeler. There was only one grade three class scheduled for 10:00 a.m., and these kids were obviously the right age.

It didn't look as though Keeler would be much of a problem. He was about thirty-five, very slim and fussy. He rushed about organizing the kids into groups of about five—gathered around an adult, probably a parent—and checking names off on a list. He must have had the lists made up in duplicate, because he handed a sheet to each parent and shuffled a second page to the bottom of his clipboard. Karen watched in satisfaction as one parent took the sheet and laughed. This guy was so insecure he probably had bathroom breaks scheduled in his day book. Perfect.

She was breathing easily now, feeling more confident. She mentally checked off the first objective.

She went to the pay phones at the far end of the cafeteria. There was no one sitting near them, and they were about as isolated as any in the building. She looked up the number of Maple Ridge Composite School, called and asked to speak to the principal. She told the secretary who answered the phone that she was Kathy Hatfield, and said she was a reporter for ClassRoom, a new magazine supplement, and that she was looking for opportunities to visit and do a photo feature on schools in the city. She was phoning to see if the principal would be willing to let her run her first spread on Maple Ridge Composite School.

The secretary said she would put her through to the principal, Mr. Melrose, and in a few minutes, Mr. Melrose himself came on the line.

"Well, this is a first for our school, Ms.... er ...Ms. Hatfield. Tell me what made you select Maple Ridge for your first article?" Herman Melrose was a promoter. Good publicity for the school was always welcome, and he was happy to listen to her proposal.

"I'm sorry," Karen said, "but I didn't get your name. Would you spell it out for me? We may as well get all the details correct before we go too far."

Herman Melrose spelled his name for her and asked again why she had chosen his school for the first article in this series.

"We're just in the planning stages, Mr. Melrose. Nothing's settled yet, but we need to check out the attitude of several schools in the city to gauge how receptive the school community would be to partnering with our company in doing a photo spread on education in the city today."

She thought that sounded pretty good. Herman thought it sounded a bit odd.

"Partnering? I'm not sure I follow you Ms. Hatfield. We often give interviews to the press and occasionally we do allow reporters into the school to do publicity shots of our sports teams and so forth, but what you're talking about sounds rather more involved. Have you discussed this with our public relations office downtown?"

There was a moment's hesitation before Karen could think of a way to get out of the hole she was digging for herself. She'd only phoned to get his name and the correct spelling, and now she had to get off the line quickly, but not so abruptly as to make him suspicious.

"What was that you said Mr. Melrose? This line is very bad. Can you hear me all right?" Still talking, she reached out and gently depressed the phone hook before replacing the receiver. He would know they had been cut off, but chances were he wouldn't suspect she had hung up on him. Step two complete.

She breathed a sigh of relief and folded her notebook and put it into her handbag. She had walked the site earlier in the week. She couldn't see the parking lot from the cafeteria, but she'd seen the buses arriving in the loading zone and she knew where to sit to check out the buses as they started to leave this afternoon.

She went back to her hotel room and unpacked her laptop and a very quiet ink jet-printer. She powered it up and printed an almost perfect replica of a court order. It purported to empower the bearer, named in larger type, Karen Hartley, Child Protection Officer of Denton City's Social Services Department, to detain one female person, name not to be released because the said person was a minor, and who forthwith would be in the sole custody of the aforementioned Karen Hartley, blah, blah, blah. The important line was in bold type: "The said officer, acting for and in the name of the Court, is hereby granted full authority to seize, detain, and transport the said minor, and the Court further charges all persons whosoever to aid and assist in any manner deemed necessary by the aforementioned Karen Hartley in the pursuit of these duties."

It was all nonsense, of course—wording gathered from legal self-help books about drawing up wills or buying and selling real estate—but it sounded pretty impressive. Most people will fold quickly if you wave a piece of official-looking paper in their face, and this was a very official-looking paper. Three court officials were named as issuing or witnessing this document. The names were real of course, but the signatures were fake. The seal she attached beside each name was simply a red peel-and-stick circular label that you can buy in any stationery store. They are still used on some legal documents and they did give the paper an added touch of phony authenticity.

She folded the document and slipped it into an envelope, a social services department envelope that she'd picked up earlier that week. It had been ridiculously easy to get. She had gone to social services, asked for an application form for social assistance and requested that they put it in an envelope because she wanted to think about it before filling it in. She had sample envelopes from every department in city hall and most offices in the courthouse. Step three complete.

She put her laptop back into its case, packed up the rest of her things and loaded everything into the trunk of her car. She went back to the room to make sure she hadn't left any bits and pieces behind. She emptied the trash and that, too, went into the trunk. It's surprising what incriminating stuff people leave in trash cans for snooping cleaners to stumble over. In the underground parking garage, she unpacked a portable flashing red light, bought earlier in the week at an auto supply store. Covering the glass with a paper bag, she plugged it into the cigarette lighter, looked around to see that she was alone and then turned it on for a ten-second test. She put it back into the box, put the box into a plastic bag and set it on the back seat. Everything was packed and loaded. She'd paid for the room in cash using the name Kathy Hatfield, and the room was paid for until tomorrow. She didn't need to check out and she still had the room for one more day if she needed it. Step four complete.

By 11:30 Karen was back in the cafeteria. She was wearing a wig, dark glasses, scruffy shoes and thick, worn pantyhose. She had a cane and a reversible coat that could be turned inside out in a second. Men still took notice of her in high heels and a tight dress, but in flat, scruffy shoes and looking years older, as she did now, she could pass for somebody's grandmother. No one gave her a second glance.

She sat by the same window, again facing the loading zone, this time to study the buses as they loaded and unloaded their passengers. A handibus waiting to load a few passengers moved along in the same line as buses unloading kids. That's how it would work this afternoon. She had expected that there would be buses coming and going everywhere, but this bus system was very well controlled. All buses, whether dropping kids off or picking them up, pulled into the zoo past the loading zone. The loaded ones turned right into a short, bus-only lane to the loading zone, dropped off their kids and then either took the right exit ramp to merge with regular traffic leaving the zoo or turned left to the parking lot to wait while the kids visited the zoo. Empty buses from the parking lot followed the same routine, merging with any incoming full buses, waiting their turn to pick up passengers at the loading zone.

The sidewalk in front of the zoo entrance was a large open concrete area, big enough to hold three or four busloads of kids coming and going at the same time. The road past the loading zone was wide enough for two buses to pass each other, but it was clearly marked for single-lane traffic. She guessed that was to allow for an emergency vehicle to get past a stalled bus and clear the lane, or for an ambulance, fire truck or whatever. It would be tricky. She would have to use the emergency lane. There was simply no other way to get close enough to get the kid away from the teacher and into her car. Once in her car it should be a simple matter to drive past the buses and out of the parking lot by the bus-only lane. As she watched, a sanding truck crawled slowly past the standing buses, spreading a layer of salt and sand over both lanes. There were large ridges of packed snow between the bus lanes, and the ice beneath gleamed black where the sand slid off the tops of the ridges.

The clock was running now and time was tight. The first problem was to get close enough to the class to pick up the name of a little girl. She didn't care which kid she got, but the contract was for a girl, about seven or eight years old, and that was her only concern. This was a fat contract, and for that kind of money they expected a clean pick-up which could not be traced back to the buyer. She could easily do one a month if she had a contract and if she moved from city to city. Not as much as she used to make in her former profession, but she didn't get slapped around nearly as much either. She didn't think much about the fate of the kids. Babies were a growth industry. They could be farmed out at incredible prices, and there were lawyers ready to facilitate their adoption by childless couples, usually rich. A little girl this age? She'd probably just disappear without a trace. But that part of it did not concern Karen. She didn't want to know. She would be glad when this one was over, but right now she had a more immediate problem to solve. She still didn't have the name of a kid in the class.

She didn't need to recognize the kid, but she would have to ask for her by name. The cafeteria would be the best place. The kids would be in soon to eat lunch here. Kids talk loud enough to wake the dead, and if she listened and walked about the room slowly, she was bound to hear at least one name and stick it to a face. Sometimes you got lucky and got a first and last name easily. Usually you only got the first name, then you had to scratch around and come up with an excuse to see the class list, or talk to the kids to get the last name, but that was very risky. Sometimes, if it was busy in the lineup and the teacher was carrying the class list—and every teacher had to have one to give to the police in case of an accident—you could just lift it, and then you had everything. But Keeler was too fussy for that. He'd know if it went missing.

The kids came into the cafeteria a little before 12:30. Most had a bag lunch or a lunch kit that they had left on the bus. The bus driver, Mrs. Miller, brought the lunches to the cafeteria and the parents distributed them, usually by calling the kid to come and get his or her lunch. By 1:30 she knew the first name of the girl she'd picked. She had no need to hang about the cafeteria any longer.

Karen had found a parking spot near the building. She retrieved her business suit from the car and went to the ladies' room to change. In less than five minutes she was dressed as Karen Hartley, again, and walking briskly back to the parking lot. No one would remember the old woman who had been in the cafeteria earlier that morning, and there was nothing to connect her with the smartly dressed Karen Hartley now leaving the building. Everything, even the face cloth she had used to remove the stage makeup that had aged her skin, was now in a nylon hold-all in the trunk of her car. She just had to keep it together for another few minutes and she would be out of there, and this job would be behind her.

She had a number to call to alert the minders that the snatch was a go and that she would be leaving the zoo within the hour.

The reception had to be ready for her and the kid. If there was no confirmation that the arrangements were in place, it was still not too late to call it off and get out. She had committed no crime here; the police would not be looking for her. But the contract would be unfulfilled, and there were people who would want to know why. So she made the call. It was answered on the first ring. She couldn't stop it now: the assurances were given. The last piece was in place. Everything she could think of was ready. It was time.

At precisely 1:45, she parked her car on the far side of the line of buses, just on the edge of the emergency lane, to avoid drawing attention to it until the kids were actually being boarded. She approached the bus, the one waiting for the kids from Maple Ridge School, and tapped on the glass panel of the door. Mrs. Miller opened it immediately. It was simplicity itself. As Karen Hartley, Child Protection Officer of the city's social services department, she asked for the class list, on official business, and found the last name for the girl Samantha. She handed the list back and stood inside the door waiting for the kids to emerge from the building. Mrs. Miller was curious to say the least, but Mrs. Hartley was so in charge, so official looking, that she'd handed over the list immediately and didn't ask her anything, although Karen stood beside her for several minutes until the kids showed up at the loading area.

Karen saw the kids coming and asked the driver to open the door. She walked smartly around the bus and back to her car, started it and drove down the emergency lane toward the bus she had just left. She jolted over the ice ruts and nosed between two buses, several buses behind the bus for Maple Ridge School. She got out, leaving the door ajar, the engine running, and the red light flashing on the dashboard to justify her car sticking out from between the two buses into the emergency lane.

"Mr. Keeler? Hello, I am so glad I caught you. I am Karen Hartley, from Social Services. My card."

It was all done in one fluid movement. She stepped up to him, addressed him by name and handed him a business card identifying her as a child protection officer from the Department of Social Services. Keeler looked dazed for a second, first trying to take in who she was and then apprehensive at the implications of being accosted by such an official here, just as his class was about to board the bus.

She waited for Albert Keeler to look up at her, and when he did she extracted the single sheet of paper from the envelope she was holding. Offering it to him she said, "Mr. Keeler, this is an authorization from Social Services. It concerns one of your students, Samantha Jensen. Her father has been injured in an accident. It's very bad, I'm afraid. Her mother is already at the hospital, but apparently there was no family member available to come for her. I've been sent to get Samantha and take her there immediately. Mr. Melrose has already been informed that Samantha will not be returning with you on the bus. Mr. Keeler, it's very important to Mrs. Jensen that I get Samantha to the hospital before it is too late. Would you call her for me? I will need a moment to explain to her what's happening."

"Well, er, Mrs....Hartley...I don't know. This has never happened before. I...er..."

"Mr. Keeler, I must hurry," she said, leaning forward and speaking in a confidential tone. "Apparently there is very little time." Gesturing to the envelope she said, "Please look over the writ. You'll find it's all in order."

Albert glanced over to where his class was lining up to board the bus and went to get Samantha. He didn't want to call out to her. It seemed more natural just to take her hand and bring her over to Mrs. Hartley. He felt she should explain why Samantha was being taken from the group and put into her car.

Karen smiled warmly at Samantha as she approached and crouched down to speak to her as intimately as possible. She took Samantha's hands in hers and went through the story again. When she finished, Samantha looked back to Albert for reassurance. Albert took her hand and told her her mother needed her and that he could not take her to the hospital. Her mother had sent Mrs. Hartley for her and she should go with her now. It was only a short ride to the hospital and her mother would meet her there.

"Thank you again for your understanding, Mr. Keeler," she said standing. "Now, is there anything else Samantha has on the bus I should take?" When Albert shook his head, she thanked him again and said goodbye. She took Samantha's hand and led her, bewildered and frightened but not resisting, to the official looking car with the portable red light flashing on the dashboard. She got in, snapped the seat belt tight around Samantha and fastened her own. She put the car into reverse, checked the mirror and started to move slowly backward. There was very little room between the buses, and the ruts were deep and slippery. She was backing out into the emergency lane, but there was no traffic and she had plenty of room behind her. The car was already moving when Albert yelled out to her.

"Mrs. Hartley!" She looked up at him as he rushed to her door. She couldn't floor it without hitting him and she still needed to go back a bit more into the emergency lane to straighten out and get out of the parking lot. No need to panic. Steady. Be calm. Smile and roll down the window, she told herself. But her hand was shaking as she pressed the button to lower the window.

He had forgotten that Samantha was on antibiotics. Some kid's always on something, and he had the pills. Erythromycin. He rushed forward before Mrs. Hartley pulled out to make sure she got the pills. He opened his coat and reached inside. Karen's eyes went wide. Her mouth was dry; her breath came in short gasps as she tensed, both hands on the wheel. She thought for one horrible second that this was a bust, that Albert was a cop and that she had been set up. But he drew out a small plastic prescription bottle and offered it to her through the open window. She relaxed a little, still on the verge of panic, and remembered to smile as she reached for the bottle.

"She's supposed to take one now," Albert said, instinctively drawing back the bottle and opening it. "I'll get her a drink. It'll only take a second. Samantha?"

And it really would only take a second. There was a fountain by the door, just a few feet away, and he intended to call her out to take the pill. Samantha understood, but when she went to release her seat belt and get out, Karen lost it completely.

She struck Samantha hard with the back of her hand, wrenched the wheel hard over right and floored it backwards, bumping Albert out of the way with the side mirror and the left front fender of the car. He was stunned but not hurt and quickly scrambled to his feet. Her wheels screamed on the icy humps until they connected with a bit of dry pavement and she shot backwards like a rocket, slewed left and into the concrete barrier at the edge of the roadway. Recovering quickly, she put the car in drive and jolted free of the barrier. She started forward, skidding again as she inched toward the centre of the emergency lane. She corrected the skid right toward the standing buses and was straightening out, but suddenly Albert lunged through the open window, fighting with her for control of the steering wheel. He knew something was dreadfully wrong. He had no idea what it was, but Albert would stop this woman from taking Samantha if it was the last thing he ever did.

Totally out of control now, with Albert clinging to the wheel, she pulled hard right against him, tires screaming on the ice, dragging him still clinging to the wheel. He was losing his grip. Karen clawed at his face to make him let go. Mrs. Miller had followed the whole scene from the bus, unable to believe what she was seeing in her side view mirror. She watched as Albert first lunged for the steering wheel through the car's open window, then slipped down the side of the car, lost hold with his right hand, his arm stretching up, trying to grasp the window frame, unable to find a hand hold. She screamed as he fell from her view down the side of the car.

With his weight suddenly gone, the wheel became soft in Karen's hands and she overcorrected too far right, slamming the passenger side of the car solidly against a bus waiting in line at the loading zone. She careened ahead for a few more feet, the metal screaming loudly until the car stopped, the bumper hung up on some part of the bus body. The much abused car stalled, refusing to go farther.

She was out of the car in a second, but hesitated, looking around for an exit. The high chain-link fence that surrounded the parking lot was as secure as a prison yard. She was miles from the centre of town, stranded without transportation. She turned back toward the buses parked in the loading zone. The first bus was empty and probably locked. The second was running and empty except for the driver, Mrs. Miller, the same driver she had conned so easily less than five minutes earlier. There was just enough room. The bus could mount the curb, drive across the wide concrete entrance area, pass the bus ahead on the inside and get out by the bus exit lane. It was her only chance.

Karen raced to the bus and vaulted through the open door. But she got no farther. What struck her square in the face was the fist of a very angry mother who drove a school bus part-time and ran a dairy farm full-time. Karen hit the floor like a side of beef and wisely decided to stay there until the zoo's security staff turned her over to the police a few minutes later. Had she tried to get up, Mrs. Miller would have decked her again in a heartbeat.

Samantha was crying and very frightened, but not hurt by the impact of the car against the bus. The parent supervisors got her out of the car and comforted her; she began to calm down as soon as she was with her friends again. She stayed next to one of the parents she knew and would not leave her until her own parents came to gather her up and assure themselves that she was safe and unharmed.

Alerted by the zoo's security service, police were on the scene in less than three minutes. They promptly had Karen Hartley in custody and moved Mrs. Miller to their cruiser to take her statement. Initially the police thought they were dealing with a simple assault and a rather bizarre traffic accident, but it didn't take them long to put the pieces together.

The zoo's security staff had seen the incident and locked down the zoo immediately. It would stay that way until the police advised them the emergency was under control. They also called

Maple Ridge Composite School to report the "accident" and to request that a teacher be sent to take charge of Albert's class. John Whitelaw, the vice-principal, had taken the call; fifteen minutes later he was escorted into the zoo.

Whitelaw walked into a scene of mild confusion and disciplined purpose. Police cars blocked every exit from the zoo. An ambulance filled the exit lane, and the paramedics were attending to Albert. Firefighters were methodically examining the damaged car and bus, checking for fuel leaks or potential fire hazards. Farther back, two big wreckers patiently waited for orders to haul the damaged vehicles away. Only Albert's parent supervisors were milling about with their charges, not quite sure what they should be doing with them. The normally busy loading zone had been cleared by the police, and the classes not involved in the incident were rapidly evacuated by way of the parking lot.

John identified himself to the police and to the parents, most of whom already knew him, and immediately took attendance with the class list he had brought from school. He could now assure the police that all the children from Albert's class were safe and accounted for. He asked the parents to take the children to the cafeteria and wait for the new driver being dispatched from the depot to come and take them back to school. Then he went to see how badly Albert was hurt.

John approached the ambulance and tapped on the door. He identified himself and asked about Albert's condition. He could see Albert strapped to a spine board on a stretcher in the ambulance. One of the paramedics stayed with Albert; the other got out to brief John on his condition. Apparently, Albert's injuries weren't all that bad. He had a broken wrist and some damage to his shoulder, but they didn't know how serious that was. He had sustained extensive bruising and had been badly battered falling from the car and rolling into the concrete barrier, but there were no signs of head injuries and no internal injuries either, as far as they could tell. He was on the spine board as a precaution, given the type of injuries he had suffered. He had deep scratches on his face, especially around his eyes. The woman driving the car had put a finger in his eye and pressed down to force him to let go. He was conscious and asked to see John for a minute. The paramedic nodded and opened the door; John climbed in.

Albert was bandaged about the head and face and both hands, and John was sure there were more bandages under the blanket covering him. "Hi Albert. It's John. How are you, buddy?"

"She fooled me, John. I let her take Samantha. She almost got away with her. Why would she do that, John?"

Albert's voice sounded strange and muffled, and the paramedic pointed to her own jaw, indicating Albert had sustained some damage to his jaw that she had not mentioned.

"Just relax, Albert. Everything's okay. The kids are fine. Samantha's safe. They're all safe and accounted for. You need to get into hospital, Albert. I'll call in and see you later, okay?"

"It was the court order, John. She had a court order to take Samantha because she said her father was in the hospital, but it's a lie. She slapped Samantha, John. Really hurt her. I had to stop her. I did, didn't I? It was a lie, John."

John put out his hand to squeeze Albert's shoulder, but the attendant stopped him.

"We're going to go now, Mr. Keeler," she said. Turning to John she added, "We really do have to go now. That court document he mentioned; I think the police have it. It was on the road near where we found Mr. Keeler, and they took it."

John went to join the kids. The emergency was over and he could have put them back on the bus to wait for the new driver. But they had been traumatized, and he needed to establish a degree of order and normalcy for them, to assure them that the danger was past and that everything was okay, now. His presence was, itself, a calming influence, but taking them to the cafeteria where they could talk their heads off while they waited for the new driver was a far better antidote to the fears that he knew they must all be feeling. And the zoo's offer of free drinks and cookies didn't do any harm, either.

Samantha's parents had arrived. One of the parents had called Bill Jensen at work and he had picked his wife up and driven her to the zoo. She was rocking Samantha in her arms, obviously far more upset than Samantha, herself, appeared to be.

Now that she was sure Samantha was safe and unharmed, Mrs. Jensen turned her fear and anger on John, demanding to know why the school had failed to provide adequate protection for her daughter, complaining loudly that somebody's incompetence and a failure to adequately supervise the children had resulted in this threat to her child.

She was very upset and he understood that, but he had no answers for her yet. He excused himself and went to circulate among the children. He assured them that Samantha was fine and that the lady who was after her had smashed up her car, but no one was hurt at all, except for Mr. Keeler, and even he was not seriously injured. Albert had looked pretty badly banged up to John, but he wasn't about to share that with the kids.

He reminded the children that what they had seen was serious and real. There are bad people out there who will hurt kids and kidnap them, and they all had to be very careful all the time. But they'd all had that lecture before, and the novelty of the adventure was already beginning to wear off.

Principal Melrose arrived, and they agreed that because John already had a handle on the situation, it made sense that he should stay to talk to the police and follow up on Albert. Melrose would ride the bus back to the school with the kids. John saw them off, then sat down with a cup of coffee for a few minutes' break before going to see if the police needed anything more from him before he left. He'd go check up on Albert at the hospital before he went home.

Bill Jensen came over and sat down opposite him. He started in on John with the same concerns his wife had raised earlier. John tried to tell him that he knew very little about what had really happened, but Bill was all wound up and going full throttle when a female voice broke in.

"Excuse me. Are you Mr. Whitelaw?"

Without turning to see who had spoken, Bill blurted out, "Can't you see we are talking, lady? We'd like a few minutes to ourselves to sort things out. Do you mind?"

"Actually, it's not 'lady'. It's Officer McCartal." Addressing John, she said, "We've taken the suspect into custody. Mr. Keeler, the teacher, is on his way to the hospital. And I just need to tie up a few loose ends before we leave the area." Turning to Bill Jensen, she said, "You're Mr. Jensen, Samantha's father. Is that right?"

She was standing in John's line of vision and he winced when Bill lost it. But Bill was quick to sputter an apology about being so upset and needing to get to the bottom of this, and so on.

Officer McCartal wasn't a bit fazed by the outburst. She pulled up a chair, sat down, put her own coffee cup on the table and fished out her little notepad before saying anything.

"Mr. Jensen, I understand you're a lawyer. Is that right?" Her notepad was on the table now and she had her briefcase open, looking for something in it before turning to him for his answer.

Bill Jensen bristled instantly. "Yes, I am a lawyer. But if you are going to warn me about not making threatening remarks, let me remind you I have a right to know what my child was exposed to and why she was so badly protected on this trip."

She found what she was looking for and placed a soiled envelope on the table before straightening up to look at him. "No," she said, "actually I was going to ask you for some free legal advice. Have a look at this." She pushed the envelope over to him and sat back to watch his reaction.

Bill scowled and picked up the envelope, drawing out the single sheet of paper inside. He scanned it and snorted in disgust.

"This is hogwash," he said. "Where did you get this? What has this to do with..." It took that long for the light to dawn. "Do you mean this...I mean...she gave this letter to the teacher and used it as authority to take Samantha? Is that what you're telling me?"

"Yup. That's what all the witnesses say happened. It fell from Mr. Keeler's pocket when he ran to grab the wheel and stop the suspect from driving away with your daughter." She took it back from Bill Jensen and handed it to John, who took it and also scanned it quickly.

Bill Jensen was quiet for a moment before he started talking, possibly just thinking out loud. "This was a planned operation. This wasn't some random act of a demented person. This was a kidnapping. But why? We're not rich. I don't understand."

Officer McCartal nodded and said, "Well, let me share a few other things with you, Mr. Jensen, and see how you react to them. I found three photo IDs in the handbag." Flipping the notepad over she said, "Karen Hartley, Kathy Henderson and Kathy Hatfield. They all show her picture and they all appear genuine to me. Also, there was a red flashing light on the dashboard, two very high quality wigs and a professional makeup kit—the kind actors use in the theater—two expensive dresses on hangers, a set of very worn clothes like most working-class women wear around the house or to the supermarket, one cane, some old pantyhose and low-heeled shoes like Grandma used to wear. Now," she said, looking up at him, "what do you suppose she needed with all those high class disguises?"

"But she used Samantha's name." Bill Jensen was visibly shaken. "Someone told me she asked for Samantha by name. I still don't understand."

"I can't explain how she knew Samantha's name, but this woman is a pro and a very well-paid one at that. She asked for a lawyer before we got anything out of her, and the guy she wants is from a big Montreal law firm. Not your average demented nut case, would be my guess. I'd bet there will be some very nervous people in lots of places tonight, worried that she might decide to tell us about who ordered the snatch and who was waiting to receive Samantha when she got out of here. And who paid for it all."

Bill Jensen needed time to digest what he had heard and he needed to revise his initial assumption that the school had been negligent in caring for his daughter. He got up and turned to leave, then stopped, turning back to John.

"About my initial blustering, John, I...er... What can I say? I apologize. It was just...well, I was so scared for Samantha, and now all this. It's too much to take in. Thank you, John." He put out his hand and John stood and shook it. Catching himself, he turned to the police officer and absently thanked her and shook hands with her too. But she didn't let go of his hand immediately.

"Mr. Jensen. I can have someone drive you and your family home. You're obviously upset and it would be best if you were not driving through rush-hour traffic just now. Or you can take a taxi. Which would you rather?"

She dropped his hand and waited for his response. For a moment John thought he was going to resist, but he just nodded and agreed to take a taxi home. Then she cautioned both of them about discussing any of the material she had shared with them. Most of it had been seen by several people, so it wasn't a secret, but it was still confidential. She didn't want any of it to become public until the police spokesperson released it to the press.

Bill mumbled his thanks to both of them again and left. John and Officer McCartal sat down. She put the envelope she was still holding back in her briefcase and closed it. Her notepad was still on the table. At length John said, "Well, I should be moving. I still have to go to the hospital and check on Albert. Is there anything else you need from me before I go?"

"Yeah, actually there is." She flipped her notepad open again and said, "I need to know a little about Mr. Keeler. Next of kin, that sort of thing, and I need you to state for the record that he is one of your teachers and that he was in charge of that class today."

They chatted like that informally until all her questions were answered and she put her notepad away. John thanked her for sharing what she knew about the kidnapping. He stood to go but hesitated, turning to her, still struggling to understand the enormity of the crime, and needing to talk about it for another few minutes.

"I can't really come to grips with this yet, you know," he said. "I can only guess what Bill and his wife are still going through. And Albert. You should have heard him in the ambulance. He blames himself for what happened, as though it was his fault he didn't see through this woman and spot her for a fraud. Not a word about himself and the beating he took trying to stop her. Did you know she drove her finger into his eye to make him let go? At least that's what the paramedic thinks happened, because of all the scratches and the blood around his eyes."

"It wouldn't surprise me," she said. "It fits with what Mrs. Miller saw from the bus. She was clawing at his face just before he fell. You do understand that he could have been killed today? And from what I saw, there was no way he could have suspected that woman was a fake. You need to assure him of that and he needs to be recognized for his rescue of Samantha."

John nodded his agreement. "You are right, of course, and it goes without saying and I'll see he gets the recognition he deserves. But what about Mrs. Miller? That was an extraordinary thing she did, too. I know her. She would never strike anyone. But when the Hatfield woman jumped into her bus, she knocked her down and held her there until the security people came and took charge of her. It's just too much to take in all at once."

Officer McCartal stood, picked up her briefcase and put it on the table. She nodded. "I know what you mean. You hear about people doing heroic things like that now and then. But you don't meet them very often." She absently pushed her chair back under the table and stood holding the back of it, looking at John for a second. Then she said, "I met two of them today. And I can't get my head around that, either."

~

The Ghost of Christmas Past

Late December, just three days before Christmas. A couple sat holding hands by candlelight across a dinner table in a small house nestled in snow-covered woods. They were clearly visible through the picture window. Decorations, both purchased and homemade, hung on the walls, and pictures drawn by little hands were proudly displayed on the windows for all to see and enjoy. It was a Christmas card that begged to be painted. The couple was having a rare dinner alone, the kids having been sent off with their grandparents the day before to start the Christmas holidays early. The teacher and his wife saying grace, giving thanks for food and family, warmth and love, everything the season could offer on this beautiful winter evening.

They didn't hear the rifle boom before the bullet shattered the window and rained glass down over the table, the food and both of them. Their eyes were closed and their heads bowed, and instinctively they continued to hold hands and bend low until the glass stopped falling.

John and Joanne Whitelaw sat at the table still holding hands, the candles now blown out along with the glass of the window, unable to comprehend what had just happened. When the glass had stopped falling, the only sound was that of a pickup roaring away down the deserted road. They sat staring at it through the broken window until its tail lights disappeared from sight. It was several minutes before they could take in the significance of what had happened, and several minutes more before they could think to call the police.

The RCMP officers arrived quickly and walked the site, but found nothing that would help to identify who had fired the shot. One officer sat with Joanne to take a statement while the other helped John nail a sheet of plywood to the outside of the window frame. They advised the couple not to sit or stand by the lighted windows for a few days and suggested that they stay indoors as much as possible.

The officers were pretty casual about it. They agreed the shot had probably come from a vehicle, likely the half-ton John and Joanne had seen driving away but couldn't describe. They were divided on the issue of the marksmanship. One officer thought that hitting the window from a moving vehicle without hitting either of them was an indication of considerable skill. The sergeant, older and more jaded than his younger partner, was of the opinion that the shooter had been so polluted that it had been a tossup whether he hit the window or shot off a toe. There would have been a bunch of them in the truck he said, and he doubted whether they even knew they'd hit the house. Both officers did agree, however, that the Whitelaws had not been the target of a serious murder attempt.

When he thought about it later, John wondered if there is a term for the opposite of a "serious murder attempt." Can you have a "light-hearted murder attempt," or perhaps a "frivolous murder attempt"? Whatever term applied, John felt the bullet through their front window was quite serious enough for him, thank you very much.

But in truth, the incident—for that was all it really was: just another incident—was not as unusual as it might seem. It was the latest in a long series of threats and insults aimed at teachers, some irritating, some spiteful, and some, like the bullet through the window tonight, downright dangerous. John and Joanne were on a Native reserve in northern Saskatchewan. The reserve had been plagued with drinking problems and social unrest for years. But even the worst places on earth have schools, and schools need principals, and John and Joanne had chosen to come to this place. And at this moment they were fairly sure that this was it—the worst place on earth.

John had been vice-principal and music director in a school in central Alberta for six years. But promotion comes slowly in city systems these days, and if his career was to advance, he needed to get some further administrative experience. His job was beginning to bore him and he could feel the lethargy setting in. He needed a challenge; while the idea of teaching in the north had never occurred to either of them, when John pointed out an ad for a principal's position on a remote reserve in northern Saskatchewan, Joanne was remarkably keen on the idea, and the kids loved it. A chance to experience the north, to ski and snowmobile, and camp out and fish in a thousand wilderness lakes—it sounded wonderful! And it was. Except that no one had told them how deeply divided this Native community was in its opinion about having non-Natives teaching in their school.

Some hated individual teachers for their condescending attitudes toward Native kids. Some simply disliked all outsiders. Most were as uninformed and indifferent to the new crop of teachers they hired each year as John and Joanne were about the people who had hired them and invited them to take up residence in their community.

John had approached his job on the reserve with an open mind. He expected it would work out. It always had back in the city. But he was woefully unaware of the friction between the Native community and the existing staff. At his first staff meeting, after the introductions were finished, he raised the question of what goals they had and what they hoped to accomplish with the students in their classrooms in the coming year. Understandably perhaps, the three probationary teachers fresh from Teachers College didn't have a clue what he was talking about. When the older, returning staff did finally respond, they made a joke of the whole topic. He had never encountered that reaction in a planning session before and he pressed them to identify something, anything that they hoped to achieve in the coming year. Then one of them expressed what they all obviously felt. Survival was priority number one here, and if John didn't already know that, he would come to understand it in the next few months. It seemed to John that implicit in the teacher's tone was the suggestion that he wouldn't last long in the job anyway, so the answer really didn't matter much.

School started on September 6th, and on the 7th, and on the 8th, and so on for the next several weeks. Kids would drift into a class for a week or two and then disappear for a couple of weeks, only to reappear again for a while. The curriculum was a joke. There were some concessions to Native studies, but most of the proposed activities were artificial and made little sense to him and none at all, apparently, to the kids.

A growing sense of frustration filled the school as well as John's personal life. Then, early in November, the first teacher came to him and told him she was leaving. She had been harassed by a few teenagers and she didn't like the mood she felt in the community. Other teachers said they felt intimidated and some had actually been threatened as they went to and from school, usually by young adults or teens no longer in school. There were drunks on the streets and fistfights were common. Domestic violence and abuse were an everyday fact of life. Solvent sniffing among young kids was rampant; that and a shocking number of suicides gave the reserve one of the highest per capita mortality rates in the country.

Morale among his staff was very low, and attendance at school was so sporadic that any consistent teaching was nearly impossible. John had to do something. So he went to the local priest to ask his advice about how they might establish some rapport with the kids, and how the school could become more acceptable to the community. The priest listened to his tale of woe, but had nothing to tell him. He was busy with congregations in a number of communities. He knew everyone, to be sure, but as a spiritual advisor, not as an educator, and he had no idea what John wanted from him.

Arnold Samson was a Métis married to a local Native woman. He had the only service station in the settlement and he'd run it for thirty years. He should have been a valuable source of information and help to John, but he wasn't. He was the biggest bootlegger in the area, though no one told John that, and he had no time for the school or meddling outsiders who threatened to upset the life of the community, such as it was.

John went to the local detachment of the RCMP, and they were about as friendly as the rest of the community. A potbellied constable, obviously finishing an undistinguished career in this northern backwater, told John to leave well enough alone. The officer was blunt and to the point. The people here were not going to change, he said. The kids could see no point in going to school and they only went because it was warm and they did some interesting things from time to time. Besides, he said, they had to have a place to meet their friends when the old man was sleeping off a skinful. He sounded contemptuous, but possibly it wasn't contempt. Maybe, John thought, he simply shared the same frustration and lethargy that infected the whole reserve and his teachers.

The manager of the Hudson's Bay store was even more strange than the other local adults John had met so far. He kept a pistol—one from stock, not one licensed in his own name—in his apartment above the store. There were bars on the inside of the windows and shutters to protect the glass on the outside. He only opened the store for a few days a week because, he said, there was no demand until the welfare cheques came in. He had no idea what made the local community tick and he cared even less. John's visit to him was a waste of time.

John went to the next settlement to seek out the Anglican cleric who ran a school there and rake over the story again with him. The minister was very young, and he and his wife welcomed John and Joanne like long-lost cousins. They found they had many things in common. The most obvious was that they were both principals, but the cleric, Robert Anderson, was in charge of one of the few residential schools left in the north. Residential schools, whether run by government or by one of the religious denominations, had a bad reputation in the Native community, and by and large, the reputation was well deserved. A school community run on semi-military lines, as most residential schools had been, with severe discipline for infractions of rules the children did not understand or respect, was like a prison to them.

That this was a healthy, functioning school complex was obvious. The current practice of involving the community in all aspects of the school, especially on matters of discipline and the rights of the students, had justified the effort the authorities had put into the program. But the necessity to bring children from a large area to such schools was fast disappearing. Most Native families demanded the right to educate their children in their own communities. Unless this school became a residential district high school, or some type of community college, John could see that its days were numbered. And while it was good to talk to the Andersons and enjoy a friendly visit, John got no real insight into why the school he was running was so unpopular.

The next week John lost another staff member, a math teacher named Tony Estrada. The teacher's wife, Maria, had been in the Bay when a fight broke out between two women. Both were obviously drunk, and one appeared to be accusing the other of messing with her husband. She had watched in horror as the women punched and kicked viciously at each other until one of them fell. The other continued to kick ineffectually, struggling to maintain her balance. No one did anything. The manager of the Bay was content to call the police, push them both out the door and close the store an hour early.

In minutes the police were there and settled the issue quickly. Neither woman appeared to be in need of immediate medical attention. The officers simply handcuffed them to secure points at either end of the van and left them to attend to other business in the settlement. There was quiet for a moment, until one of the women had the energy to start screaming again, and the van rocked as they kicked out at each other.

According to Tony, as Maria turned to go, she realized she was in the centre of a small knot of women who had gathered behind her as she paused for a moment to watch the drama of the two women in the van. One woman spat on her. She shrank back in disbelief. They closed in on her. Maria tried to push through to her car, but they blocked her path. She dropped her purchases and fled back to the Bay, but the manager had locked the door and would not answer her frantic pounding on the security gate.

Then, as suddenly as it had begun, it ended. The two officers reappeared, helped her pick up her purchases and walked her to her car. The little crowd of women melted away. That night Tony informed John that, although he himself would stick it out to the end of the month, Maria and kids were driving home to Edmonton the next morning.

The school continued to function, after a fashion. The community was a battle zone, and when the kids did come they were quiet and apparently shy. They would colour a bit, or listen if you read to them, but they would do little else. John tried to start a music program. He took money from the school budget and ordered a class set of recorders. The kids seemed genuinely interested in the whistle-like instruments for a while. They tooted them for a period or two and then lost interest in them, like everything else.

When he was down to six teachers from his original fifteen, John decided to do the unthinkable. They would visit the parents of every kid in the settlement and ask for parental support. He called a staff meeting for 8:00 a.m., left the classroom aides in charge of the kids as they arrived and told them school would start at 9:00 as usual. But when the meeting went on past 10:00, he simply didn't care. They were not sure where everybody lived and none of them had ever visited a child at home before, but they had few options left. The school was dying. The population was shrinking day by day. Hostility toward teachers was increasing. The authorities would be coming in for an inspection and evaluation of programs at the school sometime in the new year, and if things got any worse, they would all be out of a job. They had nothing to lose.

The teachers planned the project the way an army might plan a midnight raid on an armed camp. They got the kids to paint a large map of the settlement. It was a cooperative venture and quite popular with the kids. Individual classes also made their own maps, and John thought the more the better. After the roads were marked off, teachers had the kids identify each large building in turn: the school, the post office, the RCMP detachment, the Bay, etc., and finally the garage, which every kid knew and seemed to pinpoint easily. Every house was drawn in and marked with the names of every person who lived there. Several names showed up on different houses because, the children said, some people lived there sometimes and sometimes they didn't. It took three weeks to complete the maps and to ensure that they had every house located and identified.

Monday morning they told the town kids to go home before lunch. The bus kids were left in the care of the only woman teacher on staff and the two local women who worked as classroom assistants. The teachers told their students that they would be around to visit every one of their parents to show them what the kids had been doing in school. There were three hundred town kids nominally enrolled in the school, but families of five and six kids were not unusual, so the task was not as daunting as it might at first have appeared.

It took two days. The hardest part was finding a bathroom after the innumerable cups of tea that parents urged on them. But it worked. The kids were pleased to have the visits, and every teacher found something flattering to say about the kids' work or found ways to include the kids in some of the general projects that were finished in the school. If nothing else, they could say that they had missed the kids in class recently and wanted to be sure they would be coming back soon. Like parents everywhere, the community was pleased that the teachers had finally shown some interest in their kids.

They had a much larger school population in the last week before the holidays, but with so few teachers left, it was exhausting. Those were good days; they really seemed to be getting somewhere with the kids. They made decorations for the windows. The kids understood about symbolism and, when encouraged to make drawings based on symbols from their own tradition, they took to it with enthusiasm. The classroom assistants got caught up in the enthusiasm. They worked with the kids, helping them explain the stories behind the traditional symbols that they drew and coloured and carefully folded to take home.

When someone tentatively suggested a games day and an informal party for the last day before the holidays, John approached the two assistants for their reaction. They were cautious, but thought it might be a good idea and promised to help organize some food and get some adults to help supervise the party. A group of mothers from the community came and brought bannock and made tea, and John raided his freezer for a dozen cans of frozen lemonade mix for the kids. And in a gesture that touched him more deeply than he would have expected, some of the teachers' wives brought cookies or treats of some kind and they stayed to celebrate with the kids and their parents, meeting them for the first time. It could have been a school party anywhere, but it was here in this hostile place and it was a breakthrough, or at least a crack in the wall that separated them.

John's parents had come up for a visit a few days earlier, and when they left they took their grandchildren back with them to Regina for the holidays. John and Joanne would drive down when school closed on Friday, December 22. They had hoped to leave early Friday morning, but by Thursday afternoon the road south was closed by a blizzard that was now reported to be tracking north toward the settlement.

It was dark and they were about to enjoy a pleasant dinner alone on Thursday evening when the quiet was shattered by the single shot; it ruined the holiday and scared the life out of both of them. For the rest of the evening they vacuumed the rug, searching for the tiniest shards of glass. Then they sat in the dark until it was time to go to bed. All Friday they moped about inside, checking the weather reports, but the road south was still blocked.

By Saturday morning they had run out of things to do and were beginning to get on each other's nerves. Finally, they packed a lunch, put the skis in the car and headed west out of the settlement, looking for a snowmobile track to follow. They found one about three miles out, far enough to feel safe from the groups of young men who hung about the settlement on the weekend. They unpacked the skis and started down the track at a leisurely pace. They were in no hurry. The day was bright and the woods and snow were refreshing after two miserable days inside in the half-light created by plywood over the windows. They were uneasy, but not really afraid. The shot had been a statement, not an attempt on their lives. And they didn't intend to say out very long.

They had not talked at all for a mile or more when Joanne called John to look at the sky. It was noticeably darker, a thin wisp of cloud obscuring the sun in advance of the blizzard they had been warned to expect. They had been skiing for only an hour or so, but that was enough, especially if the weather was about to turn nasty. It was colder now and the going on the snowmobile track was very fast: when the temperature drops, the skis glide easily, leaving no marks on the hard-packed snow.

Finding their way out of the bush was simply a matter of following the track back to the road where the car was parked. They felt uneasy about the colour of the sky and the increase in the force of the wind. Snow began to fall and blow across the path. The track was almost a foot deep, and they were unlikely to stray off it, even in the dark, but suddenly it had become very important to get back to the car.

They travelled quickly; the wind was picking up by the minute, and the snow was now driving in on them. Visibility was reduced, but it was still clear for several dozen yards ahead. At length, Joanne called to John to stop for a moment. She was winded, or so she said. After a minute she voiced what both of them had been thinking: the trail going back seemed a good deal longer than the trail coming in had been. The fear that they had somehow left the original track and entered a second track that might run for miles in any direction began to gnaw away at them.

There was a flash and a rattle ahead. An aluminum pie plate with a nail attached was clattering and fluttering in the breeze—a lure for a lynx. There must be some kind of trap or counting device below the plate. John had seen the film presentation of just this sort of setup, used by Lands and Forests in a survey of the lynx population. But if this was the trail back out, how had they failed to see the lure when they'd passed it coming in less than an hour earlier and in broad daylight?

They continued on down the track for another few hundred feet until John called a halt. From the look on Joanne's face, she shared his suspicion that somehow they had wandered off the original track. Their only hope was to retrace their route to the place where they had turned around and start their search again. The skis had made large indentations when they stepped out of the track to turn and head back to the car, and at least they would be able to identify that spot and, from there, hopefully, find where they had wandered off the right track.

It was darker now. And colder—uncomfortably cold as they hurried back over the track they had just covered, looking for the pattern of cross marks where they had initially turned around. Half an hour later Joanne called out excitedly that she could see the pattern. They stopped and examined the marks with relief. Yes, they had found the spot where they had turned around. But in finding this place they had still not seen a second track, the place where they had turned onto the wrong track initially. They turned again. They had no other choice.

The going was slower now because the fresh snow was drifting into the track, and they were desperate to find the turnoff that they had now missed twice. They crept along, scanning the snow for the missed turn, feeling their way along the track, the light fading as the storm intensified.

There was nothing around them but the distinct outlines of the closest trees; those just a few feet off the track were now only shadows. They were in trouble. They both knew it and they were downright scared. They were cold and tired and they felt the first stirrings of panic. Suddenly, Joanne gestured toward something ahead, a light perhaps, or maybe even a snowmobile coming down the track. But it was only an aluminum pie plate on a piece of string, blowing in the wind.

There was no denying the panic now. They had seen the lynx lure twice now in poor visibility. How could they have missed it if they had passed this way in broad daylight?

They were lost and without shelter in a driving snowstorm. Panic came rolling up from deep within, and they threw themselves down the track past the lure, past the place where they had turned before, praying that the car would miraculously appear.

Exhaustion overtook them at last, and they stopped because they could go no farther. John held Joanne and she started to cry, but he shook her gently. Tears could freeze and they would do no good at this point. What kills you are the stupid things you do in the grip of panic. But if you resist the panic, you can begin to think rationally again. They had heard about people digging themselves into a snowbank and surviving until a storm blew itself out, but the thought of digging with their hands into the snow and willingly crawling into it was too much for either of them.

It was while they were gasping for breath, shaking with the cold, that Joanne saw the boy standing in the trees, just looking at them. John was still holding her, trying to comfort her, when she stiffened in his grip and tried to pull away from him. For a second he thought she was about to go blundering wildly off, but she only raised her arm and pointed over his shoulder. He turned to see what she was pointing at.

He would have missed the boy in the darkness if Joanne had not pointed him out. They stood transfixed, startled for a moment by the sudden appearance of this lone figure. Then relief flooded over them. It seemed so improbable that a boy would be there, but they were, after all, only a few miles out of the settlement and a mile or so from the road. Someone must live out here, or be travelling, just as they were.

"Hello," John called through his teeth, his breath coming in great gasps. "We've got ourselves lost. Can you point us back to the road?"

The words came in jerky bursts. John knew he was in an advanced stage of hypothermia and fast losing his ability to control his shivering. The figure appeared to be a young boy all alone out here in the middle of a snowstorm. He didn't seem to move, but they could see him more clearly now, as if he had come closer to them. His words, when he spoke, were understandable but somehow indistinct, distant. He seemed to be saying, "I go my fawder trapline. I don't go dat school no more." The boy was looking toward them, but he wasn't addressing them. It was if he was talking to someone else, but there was no one else there.

He wasn't a student John recognized, and John didn't understand what he was saying about the school. He decided he was too cold to think clearly and returned to the only thing that mattered. They had to get this boy to help them.

"Do you understand we're lost? We need help. Can you take us to our car? It's out on the road." The boy did not move. He did not speak. After a moment John called out again, "Do you live nearby? We have to get warmed up. Will you take us to your place? Please, will you help us?"

The boy moved toward them in the snow, not using the track, starting back the way they had come. The drifted snow must have been harder than it looked, for he didn't sink in and he left no track on the crust. He still seemed unaware of them, but he spoke again as he passed them. John heard him distinctly this time, or thought he did, and he repeated aloud: "I go my fawder trapline. I don't go dat school no more." Joanne looked at him quizzically, and John said, "Didn't you hear that? That's what he said. I'm sure I didn't imagine it. Look, he's moving. We have to keep up with him."

Awkwardly, they turned and started after him, back down the track again. He was a little ahead of them when he paused to look up into a tree. A rabbit hung on a cord, and following his gaze down, they could make out the outline of a huge bear trap, the old-fashioned kind with pointed saw teeth at least two inches long, spring loaded, open and deadly, and covered with a dusting of snow and a few spruce branches over the edges.

But it was the wrong time of year for bear. And nobody trapped them any more. You couldn't eat them because they fed on the garbage from the settlement, and you couldn't legally sell any of the parts; at least John didn't think there was a bootleg trade in bear parts in this area. The trap didn't make any sense, and stranger still, they must have stopped and stood just about here twice already, looking at the lynx trap, and they hadn't seen the rabbit hanging in that tree either time.

The boy moved past the trap and continued back the way they had come, and they followed him as fast as they could. He moved quickly, seemingly indifferent to the cold and the growing darkness. They struggled to keep up, afraid to lose him but puzzled by his behaviour. They overtook him and called to him, but if he heard them, he gave no sign of it. They were abreast of him now and moving with him, not three feet away, on a parallel course. And still he did not look at them or acknowledge their calls for help.

John studied the boy with a growing sense of unease. He was very slight and not more than thirteen or fourteen years old. He had a slouched cap pulled down over his forehead, an old cloth cap like the ones gangsters wore in movies from the thirties. His coat was made from a blanket—white, with two thin, dark stripes at his shoulders—held together with several large buttons and a pin of some sort, totally inadequate for this cold weather. His pants flared at the pockets and then cut in tight round the calf. They were far too short for him and his bare legs were exposed for a couple of inches above his ankle-high black leather boots. He appeared to have no socks or gloves, but he kept his hands deep in his pants pockets. There was something decidedly strange about his whole appearance.

Suddenly, he stopped and stared toward them, or possibly past them. Again, he seemed to be speaking, but if he was, John heard nothing this time. The boy turned, gestured vaguely down the track and, without a further word, walked into the trees and was gone. John panicked. He flung himself after the boy, determined to follow him into the trees, but he floundered, his skis sank in the deep snow and he fell. He was fumbling in panic now, trying to unclip his skis and follow the boy. Joanne called to him, but he was so intent on tearing at his skis with his numb fingers that he didn't hear her until she struck him with her ski pole, hard, in desperation, three or four times.

"There," she yelled, pointing down the track. "There," she repeated again and lurched down the track, leaving John to struggle up on his skis and follow her. He had to catch her, now only a few feet ahead of him but already disappearing into the storm. Then he, too, saw it: a sliver of yellow light just visible in the snow and something dark up ahead. He overtook Joanne just as she reached the door of the cabin. The dark snowmobile was almost covered in snow, and the track it had made, the one they had been following, was all but obliterated as the snow drifted in to fill it. She slumped against the door, banging feebly on it. He caught her under the arms and pulled her up, calling out to the people in the cabin. The door opened and he fell over her. Hands pulled him upright, someone unclipped his skis, and he was lowered gently to the cabin floor. Someone got Joanne in and closed the door; for a long moment they just lay on the floor, too exhausted to take it all in.

They ripped open the Velcro flaps and pulled his ski jacket off. He assumed they were doing the same for Joanne. He couldn't see clearly yet, but someone helped him to sit up and someone else held a mug of hot, sweet tea and helped him to drink. His breath came in great gasps and he had to pause between gulps of tea to avoid choking. The room was stifling. There were perhaps five adults and three or four kids of various ages sitting on the floor beside him, feeling his jacket or playing with the Velcro flaps on the pockets and with whatever they found inside. Joanne was beside him. He reached out and held her and she sank into his arms, still shuddering, he could not tell if from the effort to get her breath or with sobs of relief. There was a general undertone of humour each time someone laid a hand on his shoulder to offer him another cup of tea, and the kids broke into howls of laughter when Albert—he thought it was Albert Cardinal from grade three—put his jacket on and curled up on the floor, shaking and moaning, "Help me, help me."

Joanne handed back her empty mug with thanks, and slumped into him; he held her for a long moment. Eventually, he rolled away from her and they sat looking up into the circle of faces above them. They were not malicious, but they were enjoying the joke in their own quiet way. The high and mighty principal in his brand-new city clothes sitting on the cluttered floor thanking God he found you, when he only lived a half mile farther down this same road.

All the energy seemed to have drained out of him. He gratefully accepted another mug of steaming hot tea, this time with a generous dollop of something that smelled suspiciously like rum, on a reserve that by law was dry.

John knew where they were. They had done a circle and come into the settlement from the other side, not more than six or seven miles as the crow flies from where they had first picked up the snowmobile track. Yes, they had been in serious danger, the kind of danger a baby would be in if you set him out on the back porch naked after his bath, just an arm's length from safety. Which was just about how John felt now, sitting on the floor in his neighbor's tiny cabin, the centre of attention.

He could hear the quiet voices of the older people talking in their own language, occasionally chuckling, and he knew they were talking about him. This really was the end. He was finished as principal here now, and good riddance. His mind had been made up for him. What had driven them out was not hostility from these people, but his own awareness of how foreign he was in this community. They didn't belong here. It was as simple as that. He knew nothing of their customs or language and he could never hope to earn their trust now. They would be too busy chewing over this story and laughing to take him seriously again. Honestly trying to do your job is not enough if you can't figure out what that job really is and if you make a monumental ass of yourself in the bargain. Well, what's the point?

Harry Cardinal, one of the older teenagers no longer in school, looked into his face and said softly, "So, you was just out for a little walk in the snow, eh?"

The laughter exploded again, and he acknowledged Harry's joke with a grin and a tilt of his mug of tea. John shook his head in self-rebuke, and he and Joanne joined in the laughter. Why not? It was funny, now that they were safe and warm inside. Even the embarrassment had faded somewhat in the general humour of the situation.

The laughter subsided. The conversation slowed and then stopped. The kids were all gathered around them, looking expectantly at them. The adults were quiet too, not smiling exactly, but regarding them more with indulgence than humour, knowing perhaps better than they themselves did how close it had been.

Joanne glanced at John and he read her query. Was it time to go? Is that why the group had now gone so quiet? He didn't think so. They were very attentive, still looking at them as if waiting for something more from them. There was an awkward pause that John couldn't read, and they just sat for another minute, unsure what to do next.

Albert Cardinal, sitting on the floor beside John, plucked at his sleeve. He asked, "How come you got lost and come t'our house?"

There were a few quiet chuckles, and he suddenly realized that's what they were waiting for. They wanted to hear the rest of the story. He could picture what he and Joanne must have looked like, blundering into their home, shivering and nearly incoherent with the cold. So how did they come to get lost and, stranger still, how did they come to stumble into this house? And more to the point, how could he tell these people with a straight face that they'd lost their way and ended up going back and forth in the same snowmobile track until they were sure they were going to freeze to death? He flushed with embarrassment and shrugged helplessly at Joanne.

"Go on," she said. "The children want to hear about our adventure in the snow and how we nearly got turned into two big ice cubes."

She was smiling at him and he understood immediately what she was saying. He gave her a hug and a peck on the neck. He drew her close to him so that they faced the children. It was story time. They were both teachers and they were about to engage an audience of children again, as they had done countless times before. They would speak to the children, knowing the adults would follow and enjoy the story, as they always did.

John started with the cleanup from the broken window, not the gunshot. Joanne exaggerated the search for the tiny shards of glass in the rug. In seconds the kids were giggling and patting the floor with her, looking for bits of imaginary glass. Then there was the boredom from doing housework and the need to get out for some fresh air. The decision to go for a short ski in the sunshine brought fresh giggles from the kids, and they were well into the story in minutes. It flowed out of them like the lines of a well-rehearsed play, and they handed off the lead to each other effortlessly.

John was enjoying himself, exaggerating the details of the penetrating cold, the menace of the gathering storm and their indecision about which way to proceed. The kids were caught up in the drama of the story, their eyes widening in suspense as he described the flash and rattle of the lynx lure, sighted not once, but twice, confirming that they were now hopelessly lost.

Joanne could not pass off so lightly the reality of the danger they had been in or how serious their situation had been, but she was content to let John tell the story and grateful she was now only a bit player in the performance.

Then, suddenly and without warning, it all fell apart. John told about seeing the figure of the boy in the shadows. It was too dark to see him clearly, John said, but he just appeared out of nowhere and pointed them down the track toward the Cardinals' cabin. Then he slipped back into the bush and was gone. It took a few minutes for John to realize that he had lost his audience. He was telling about coming into their cabin, attempting an exaggeration of the situation, but the humour was lost on the audience. He sputtered to a stop, unsure what had broken the spell, unsure why the mood had changed so abruptly and become serious.

There was silence and no one said a word for several minutes. An old woman sitting at the back of the room finally broke the silence. She spoke so quietly that John couldn't make out what she was saying. She wasn't speaking to John. She said, *"I dreamed of Matthew last night. I haven't thought of him in many years, but I dreamed of him last night."*

At last John looked at Harry and asked, "What did she say? I couldn't make out what she was saying."

"She is very old, my grandmother. Sometimes she just talks to herself. She doesn't speak much English."

Another long pause and then she spoke again, in Cree, John supposed. He just knew it wasn't English. *"He said he was very cold, and he said his friends were with him."*

Again John looked at Harry, and after a few moments Harry spoke.

"She wants to know about that boy. She wants you to tell her about him, did he have some friends with him, and what did he look like?"

John was acutely aware of the silence in the room. "I don't know what I can tell you about him," he said. "We didn't recognize him and we didn't see anyone else with him. But when the boy spoke he seemed to be talking to someone else, somebody we didn't see. It was very eerie. It was like..." He paused, struggling for a suitable description. "I don't know. Like he didn't even know we were there."

John noticed that Harry was not translating what he said for his grandmother. Perhaps she understood more English than she could speak. She was speaking again and John waited for Harry to translate.

"They all came this far together. Then they went back and he went on alone. Ask him what he said. Ask him if he saw where Mathew was going."

Another long pause. It seemed to John that Harry was reluctant to translate for her or, more likely, reluctant to tell Joanne and him what she was actually saying. Eventually he said, "She says maybe he was talking to his friends and they didn't see you. Did you hear what he was saying? Did the boy say where he was going?"

"He said something about never going back to school, wherever that was, and going to a camp, a hunt camp I suppose. Then he just sort of turned and went back into the bush."

Joanne put her hand on John's arm. She sensed they needed to hear more about the encounter, and she knew John was being deliberately vague.

"Harry," she said, "tell your grandmother that it was the strangest thing we have ever experienced. Tell her that when the boy came to us, he was just standing in the shadows, not moving at all, and we could just barely make him out in the darkness. Tell her that when we called out to him to help us, he didn't react or look at us or anything. But he came toward us and then moved past us back toward your house, and when he moved we followed him. Tell her that he didn't seem frightening or anything, just intent on going wherever he was going. I don't think he even knew we were there."

She paused, waiting, John guessed, for some reaction to what she had said. Harry turned to his grandmother and spoke briefly; she said something just as brief in return. He turned and looked at Joanne and said, "She says she understands you. She says maybe you can describe him, that boy. There's a story the old people tell about a boy who got lost in the woods near here and died. She says maybe you can describe that boy."

John was surprised that the focus had shifted to Joanne from him. He thought it was probably that the two women were sharing something between them that excluded him. Men do the same thing, talking among themselves, excluding women from the conversation and not even aware that they're doing it. So it was good Joanne was here to speak to her for them.

"We skied along beside him for several hundred yards," she said. "He walked on the snow and was very close to us, but he never looked at us. He was not dressed for the cold. Leather boots with no socks and bare legs, old-fashioned pants tight around the calf and flaring out by the pockets." She made a gesture with her hands describing the pants ballooning out. "With a blanket made into a kind of coat and a thick, heavy cloth cap with a short brim, not a long one like a baseball cap, but short. Do you understand?"

Harry turned to his grandmother. She nodded and said, "*Their camp was near here, over by the stream, but the family wasn't here yet and he froze to death. Ask them what he said. He didn't talk Cree no more. They beat it out if him. Ask them again.*"

Harry turned back to Joanne. "She understands. She wants to know what he said. How did he talk when you heard him?"

"I heard him talk," Joanne said, "but I couldn't tell what he was saying. You heard him, John. Tell them what he said."

John had tried to avoid this. He was afraid to repeat the words for fear of offending them with his pronunciation. But Joanne would not let it go. She was holding his gaze, and he would have to attempt it. "Well," he said, "it sounded like, 'I don't go that school no more. I go my father's trapline'." He said it without inflection and in a monotone, but in repeating it he remembered that it was a trapline and not a camp the boy had said he was going to. He repeated it more quickly the second time, putting an inflection into the voice and with more confidence. "I go my fawder trapline. I don't go dat school no more."

The old woman spoke again. *"It was him. That's how we dressed back then, in the stuff they gave us. It was how he looked back then. They seen him. Tell them they seen him."*

Harry spoke to her gently and they carried on a quiet conversation. John heard Harry say "No" several times, quietly but insistently, and saw him place his hand on her shoulder in a gesture of affection.

Finally Harry turned to them and said, "She is very tired and I told her she needs to go to bed. She knows, but she likes to listen to you talk. But maybe you're okay to go home now? She would go to bed maybe after you go. She gets too excited when there are too many people around."

"I am sorry if we tired her," Joanne said quickly. "I hope it wasn't too much for her. We're fine to go now." Oddly, she wanted to say something about how comfortable she felt in their home, or that she didn't understand why they had felt so isolated from the community until now, but she didn't. It would have sounded foolish.

John got up, thanked them all for their kindness again and gathered up their gear. There were little jokes, like was he sure he could find his way home along the road, and how a little farther down the road they should see the lights from his own house, and someone said they could come back if they got lost again. They all laughed, even Harry. The mood had lightened considerably. They got to the door and John paused. They had expressed their thanks and there was nothing more to say, but still he hesitated. When he spoke it was as much of a shock to him as to any of them.

"There was a bear trap out there. There was a rabbit on a cord hanging from a branch as bait, right over a hideous old bear trap. He showed us that too," he said. Joanne mumbled another thank you and closed the door. They kicked into their skis and left. They were home in fifteen minutes.

Joanne got ready for bed. She ran a tub of hot water to soak in for a few minutes, desperate for clean sheets and a few hours of blessed, quiet sleep. John made a cup of coffee and sat staring into it. The steam stopped rising from the cup. The house was quiet; even the sound of the furnace seemed muffled and distant. Joanne came out to join him at the kitchen table in a faded bathrobe, her hair in a towel, because she was too tired to use the hair dryer. She sat, and they held hands. Neither of them could sleep.

It felt as though a thunderhead was about to burst, the deafening boom of thunder long overdue. Light from the school parking lot seeped in through a crack between the frame and the plywood cover. John counted the outdoor lights as they came on. They were all on now. He walked to the kitchen window and removed the heavy blanket they had tacked up earlier. It wouldn't be needed any longer.

He watched as the lights went on all over the school. It was a community school, and many groups had access and the right to use the building, but none were scheduled to be in the building at this time of night. Joanne joined him and they watched the cars and trucks arrive. The people drifted slowly into the building. Someone came toward the house. Harold had seen them standing in the window, backlit in the light from the bathroom. He came and stood outside, looking up at them. He beckoned to them to come out. It took a few minutes to dress, but when they came out he was still there to walk with them across the parking lot and into the school.

The gym was full of people, standing and sitting, talking and visiting. They had pulled the chairs out from under the stage area and stacks of chairs were piled against the wall, people taking them as they needed them.

Harold took them to where his family was seated, and John and Joanne sat down among them. The children grinned up at them again, and Albert climbed up to sit beside Joanne; she cuddled him as she would have cuddled one of her own children.

The stove in the little kitchen had huge pots slowly heating on the burners and in the oven. The big 40-cup perks were full and the ready lights glowed red on two of them. Most of them would be full of hot water, of course. Tea, rather than coffee, was the drink of the gatherings, and they drank gallons of it. And when the food was ready, they ate. They ate until they stopped. They talked until they stopped, and then they did it all over again.

The conversation died for a while when the police constable entered the gym and walked around, sniffing the pots and peering into the corners of the room. He found a pot of coffee, got a cup and sat with John and Joanne for a few minutes before leaving, obviously bewildered by the unscheduled gathering. And then they started talking again.

A drum began beating softly. Dancers arranged themselves in a circle and moved slowly to the rhythm of the beat, whispering a chant. The Whitelaws hadn't a clue what the chant was about, but when the dancers came and led them to the circle, they joined in and thumped about as best they could. It went on until it stopped. Then everyone cleaned up, put the chairs and pots away and went off as if by arrangement, in little groups of three or four. Eventually, John and Joanne went home too, but first they turned off most of the lights and locked the doors so they could be alone in the building for a little while.

At the back of the office area in the school was a storage vault, like a walk-in closet but with a heavy steel door. It had been old when the building was renovated thirty years earlier, but no one had seen any reason for ripping it out. In it the accumulated history of the settlement resided: boxes neatly labelled in five-year increments, school records tied in dusty collections with the registers and the minutes of the official meetings between the government representatives and school administrators. It only took a few minutes to locate the registers and the administrative logs from the residential school that had been closed and torn down in 1939.

Joanne suggested that they start with 1939 and work backwards. She was sure the boy's clothes were typical of the 1930s and that they would likely have shown up in donations distributed on the reserve by the late 1930s. The records were very thin, and they skimmed through them quickly, until they found a reference to a police investigation into the deaths of a group of boys from the school at Christmas in 1938. The report had been tabled at a special meeting of the school administration in January of 1939.

According to the report, sometime during the evening of December 24, 1938, when security had been lax because several of the staff had returned south to spend Christmas with relatives, six boys, residents of the school, ranging in age from seven to thirteen, all "noted troublemakers," had left the institution without permission. After breaking the lock on the pantry door and stealing a small quantity of food, they had forced the lock on the dormitory door and made their exit over the institution's south fence. It was very cold. They had taken their outer clothing and had foolishly attempted to walk the twenty or so miles to a temporary campsite used by the family of one of the boys when trapping in the area. This information had been volunteered by other students at the school. The searchers had established that the boys had travelled as a group for some eight or nine miles, when all but one of them had turned and apparently attempted to retrace their route back to the school. All of them had perished. The one boy who had continued on alone had actually walked to the campsite, but it had been deserted, and his body was discovered there. One boy had apparently stepped into a large trap and died quickly from massive leg wounds and cold. The report did not speculate on why a bear trap was set so late in the year, nor did it identify the person responsible for setting it. A school administrator had added a note expressing the opinion that the trap might have been intended for a wolverine, which had been tracked to the area by one of several local farmers who had seen it near their outbuildings.

A list of the deceased, with their ages and the dates on which they had been taken into the school, was attached. There was a precise statement of how each of the boys had died, and where and in what condition each of the bodies had been found. The name of the boy who had been found at the campsite was Matthew Littlefox, and the campsite itself was identified as the winter campsite of the Cardinal family. John and Joanne assumed he was the most likely candidate to be the boy in the story Harry told them about, and they went looking for more information about him.

They located the long, framed, black-and-white photos of the grim-faced boys and stern, God-fearing teachers who had done their best to beat their notion of civilization into them—in this case, obviously, without much success. The photos were mounted in cardboard folders, packed on the bottom of the carton. Each was neatly labelled by year and class, and a numbering system identified each person in the photo. Matthew Littlefox showed up in the photos for 1936, 1937 and 1938. The boots and pants were the same, but there were no photos of the boys in hats and coats. But it wasn't necessary. They recognized him immediately.

They wondered if Matthew's mother had been a Cardinal and had married someone named Littlefox, but at that point it really didn't matter. They knew enough of the story and were content to put the records away, lock the room and leave the dust to settle once again on the framed pictures of the misery from so long ago.

The weather cleared, and John got a lift to retrieve the car later in the day. They were one day late for Christmas dinner, but their parents understood about bad weather and closed roads, and their children were too busy watching television and playing with new toys to be very upset.

When they got back to the settlement after the Christmas holidays, the children attended in larger numbers than ever before. If they showed no greater inclination for punctuality, they did at least attend regularly now, and they were obviously more willing to work while they were in school. John called several of the teachers who had left before Christmas; five returned, but he was blunt about the terms on which they were coming back. A kind of truce had been struck with the community; they would be tolerated until they deserved to be welcomed, or they would leave for good at the end of term.

No magic wand was waved over the settlement to solve the massive problems that were destroying the people. But the Elders did call John to meet with them to discuss ideas for improving employment opportunities among the young people as a necessary first step in addressing the other problems in the community. Every year the government spent millions of dollars on projects all over the north, but they imported workers from the south because they said the local people lacked the skills to make them useful to the contractors. If they could be persuaded to turn the Andersons' residential school into a community college instead of closing it down, and if John's school could be expanded to accommodate all of the local high school kids and those now attending school, perhaps they could make a start on providing the young people with the job skills they needed to find employment on the reserve.

Would John be willing, they asked, to organize the research necessary to draw up a plan to take to the government ministry responsible for education and employment on the reserve and to convince them to consider the proposal? They needed a unique individual, someone respected by the community and acceptable to the ministry, and John was emerging as the only logical candidate. If the evaluation of the school was as positive as it now appeared likely to be, he would be in a very strong position to speak about the educational needs on the reserve. He could count on the band council's full support, they said, and he was the first outsider to whom they had made that commitment.

He didn't have to think about it very long. It was the first positive outreach by the Native community to deal with the long-term problems that plagued the reserve, and it made a lot of sense. Construction in the area would offer employment, at least in labouring jobs, to many of the young people on the reserve now. The new courses in basic skills would enrich the labour pool and expand employment opportunities for the future. And the experience gained in negotiations with various contractors and the government would smooth the way for the eventual takeover of the entire financial control of the reserve by the next generation of younger, better-educated Native leaders.

John had found his challenge. Joanne was not as enthusiastic as he had hoped, but considering the introduction she had had to the community, not to mention the little matter of the two-week delay in getting a new front room window shipped up and installed, she was surprisingly supportive. She would give it a try, she said, and if things did continue to improve, perhaps they could build a new life for themselves and their children among these people.

The goodwill of the community was obvious. The band council financed and built a new service station in the settlement. It sold gas and made car repairs and it did both cheaply and quite efficiently. The old garage didn't even try to compete. When the women of the community took to bringing sewing in and sitting in the waiting area to do their handicrafts, the trade in booze dried up quickly. Nobody said anything and nobody was arrested, but the owner moved on and the community became dry again. And sober. And less violent.

After a little while John and Joanne didn't talk about their strange encounter in the woods less than a mile from their own back door. What closed the matter once and for all was the shock John got in the school gym late one evening after he thought everyone had gone home. He had closed up his office and was heading out when he noticed the janitor had left the gym door open again, and he went to close and lock it. It was only about 5:00 p.m., but winter days are short in the north, and it was jet black outside. Only the night lights from the parking lot illuminated the interior of the school. There, sitting on the top step of the platform, leaning against the handrail, apparently sound asleep was Matthew Littlefox. John dropped his keys and the figure stirred and came toward him. There was the white blanket-coat held together with the safety pin and a couple of buttons. And the ankle-high black leather boots and the thick old-fashioned cap. Only it wasn't Matthew. It was a new student who had registered that morning with the secretary but whom John had not seen during the day. He had simply missed his bus and didn't know how to get home, so he had just sat on the steps in the gym and had fallen asleep. He knew someone would turn up for him eventually and he was not unduly concerned about being alone in the school. Sure enough, there was a truck in the empty parking lot, full of his family waiting to squeeze him in and go home.

~

Two Blind Mice

Commander Spock was hunched over his console. As science officer, Mr. Spock was in command of the expedition to this alien world. He demanded absolute silence as he ran his smooth hands over the input device, trying to coax a reluctant computer to merge its essence with the foreign intelligence on which their fate hung. Spock was acutely aware of Captain Kirk leaning over his shoulder, because Kirk's breath reeked of the anchovy sauce he had ordered for the pizza they had shared tonight.

"That's them, that's them!" Kirk said, excitedly waving his can of Coke in the air as the screen cleared and the logo began to form. Spock did not see the drop of fluid land on the screen or, in language most uncharacteristic for a Vulcan, he would have ordered Kirk to sit down and shut up. Their hopes soared for a moment, but the logo they sought dissolved and was replaced by the flashing message, "Access Denied."

"Yeah, it's them," said Spock, "but they've locked us out. I can't get in. We're dead."

Their worst fears were confirmed. The system had detected their unauthorized presence and closed the access loophole they had found. They had made contact just once too often—two high-school geeks playing silly games in Denton City's computer system, with no way to repair the damage they had caused. And there was no Scotty in the real world to beam them up from the mess they had created.

Jeff Kershaw and Willard Ransom had assumed their respective roles in elementary school during afternoons spent watching countless reruns of the original Star Trek episodes. Their personae had languished in junior high only to blossom afresh as hacker identities in high school. They'd watched The Next Generation, of course, and they went to each of the movies as they came out, but they were still hooked on the original Star Trek characters. Jeff saw himself as the efficient and coldly calculating Spock. Willard became Captain Kirk. Jeff had appointed Willard captain because he seemed to have no talents useful for anything on earth. Willard had assumed it was a compliment. They were as unlikely a pair as had ever assumed the mantles of their respective heroes. Jeff was tall, thin and had a prominent nose that tended to drip inconveniently at times. Willard was shorter and a bit pudgy, with a glazed expression suggesting he didn't know what was going on most of the time and probably wasn't all that concerned about knowing anyway.

It was 9 p.m. on a dark and cheerless Sunday, the twenty-eighth of November. Suitably dressed in their authentic Star Trek T-shirts, they sat in the school's overheated computer classroom frantically trying to contact the city's computer. This was a hack they had done several times before. In the past it had been simply for fun. But this wasn't fun anymore.

"We're not dead," said Willard, ambling back to his own workstation across from Jeff in the crowded computer classroom. "You probably just screwed up. Go back and get into the data files so we can fix this mess and go home." Willard's attention drifted back to the glitch in his own graphics program.

Jeff sat unmoving, staring at the screen for a long minute before turning to face Willard.

"It won't do any good. They know we're trying to get in and they've locked us out. If I try again, they'll find us for sure." Suddenly animated, Jeff said, "We have to quit now! We may still be in their system, even if it isn't printing on the screen. They could be monitoring us right now." He turned back to his computer, frantically searching for the scrap of paper with the DOS commands he needed to back them out of the program without leaving an identifiable footprint.

"Find us?" asked Willard, absently. "Find us how? Snoop and Scoop won't let them. It'll just evaporate and..."

"And they'll never know we were in? Yeah, right. But they do, don't they? That's how they knew to kick us out—because they knew we were in their data files. They were just waiting for us to come back and try again. The hack's a bust!" He found the paper he needed and, holding it flat, began pecking in the proper sequence of commands. "They know, Willard. We're dead meat! They know you killed off Mr. Scrivner and they're gonna come looking for us. Dumb, Willard. That was really, really dumb," said Jeff, staring at the screen. When the snow cleared and the crude little menu for Snoop and Scoop, their hacker tool for cracking secure systems, popped up, Jeff let out a long breath and slumped back in his chair.

"How come it's always my fault? Like, you never make mistakes, do you? Oh no. But I'm stupid because I made one little slip-up. Well, so what?" Willard paused, waiting for Jeff to respond. When Jeff didn't answer, he prompted again, "So you think, like, we could get suspended or something?" When Jeff still didn't respond, Willard asked, "Expelled? They wouldn't expel us over this, would they?"

Finally Jeff turned to Willard and said in utter frustration, "Never mind school, Willard. We're in way more trouble than that. Think police! Think criminal stuff for messing with the city's computer and what we've done to Mr. Scrivner and everything. We're in trouble, Willard. Really, really big trouble."

From his usual place in the middle aisle across from Jeff in the classroom, converted now into a crude computer lab by the addition of thirty computers and bundles of cables strung temporarily between the desks, Willard sat watching his newly created explosion spread colour across the screen and then fade to grey. All he said was "Oh." Then, after another long pause, he asked, "Do you want to split that last Coke?"

Jeff dropped his head into his hands and moaned just loud enough to be heard. What was there to say? Willard was an idiot!

They'd killed Mr. Scrivner. Well, sort of killed him. It was an accident, of course, but it wouldn't matter. They were doomed. Scrivner was a pain and accounting was worse than a visit to the dentist, but they hadn't meant to do him any harm. Not really. Not recently, anyhow.

True, they had thought about putting a bomb, just a little one, in the engine compartment of his car to let him know just how ticked off they were at him. That was last year when they had both failed Accounting 12. But the timing device had defeated them. Then Jeff had designed an ingenious tap into the high-tension lead from the ignition to a detonator, to get around the need for a timer. But they didn't actually have a detonator, or dynamite, and they wouldn't have used it if they had. So they went over to Mr. Pizza for a medium double-cheese-with-pepperoni instead.

Some people think fate maintains an extensive bureau dedicated to watching out for people like Jeff and Willard, to prevent them from applying for early membership in the hereafter through such activities as cleaning lint out of electric outlets with paper clips or sucking up puddles of Coke with a regular vacuum cleaner. They had done all that and much more, and the fact that they were both still here after several close encounters with eternity was a small wonder in itself.

As long as they confined their activities to daydreaming about bumping off Mr. Scrivner, he and they were perfectly safe. However, when they attempted to implement one of their more hare-brained ideas, no one was safe. Take, for example, the time they thought it would be possible to reverse the current through a satellite dish and use it to generate microwaves and fry him in his car. Not "fry" as in dead, of course, just "fry" as in sort of lightly toasted. They attempted to feed an AC current into the coaxial lead of the dish on the roof of the school overlooking the parking lot, but when they cut into the line nothing happened. Nothing obvious, that is, for about thirty seconds. The controls did melt, and eventually the cable shorted out, but not before Willard, who was holding the cables together with his bare hands, began picking up a heavy-metal station on the metal fillings in his teeth. The music coming from Willard every time he opened his mouth to scream so fascinated Jeff that he wouldn't disconnect Willard from the cable for a good minute or more. Willard was ticked off at Jeff for a while, but it had been a blast, and by the time the burns on his fingers healed they had pretty much forgotten all about it.

Willard decided one day that the reason Mr. Scrivner was so miserable was that he was not married. Jeff countered that Mrs. Curtis, Mr. Pendleton and Mr. Boychuk were all married, and that they were just as miserable most of the time. It never occurred to either Jeff or Willard that the common denominator among all of these occasionally unhappy people was that they were all teachers who had Jeff and Willard in their classes. Willard, not one to let go of a good idea lest it die of loneliness before he had another, decided that if Mr. Scrivner and Miss Wilmore could get together, they would find they had much in common. He bought some chocolates, half-price after Valentine's Day, and slipped them into her mailbox in the office when the secretary was alone and too busy to notice. His note pledged undying love and was signed "Mr. Scriviner." They watched Miss Wilmore take the chocolates to her room and then make a beeline for Scrivner's room. There followed a period of intense laughter that Willard interpreted as the beginnings of a deep and meaningful relationship. Jeff suggested, correctly as it turned out, that they had recognized Willard's handwriting and simply thought he was a monumental jerk. The teachers had in fact spotted Willard's unique style immediately. The dead giveaway was that he had misspelled Scrivner's name. Still, they had endeared themselves to their teachers, for it was a nice thought, even if it might appear to some people to be presumptuous, scatterbrained, insufferably arrogant and just plain dumb. It was all of those things. But in the eyes of their teachers, for Willard and Jeff, that was progress.

Thinking about torrid love affairs set them to wondering about girls. Jeff had actually had a date with a girl once. Only once, though, and neither he nor Amy Scrogens was interested in a rematch. Jeff was smart enough to realize that he was no prize, and though he was aware that Amy would never win any beauty contests, he had no idea how well she knew it. But she did, and that explains why she agreed to go out with "that geek Jeff."

Jeff and Willard hadn't the faintest idea about the female of the species. They'd had only one Health class on the subject of sex that year, a lecture given by Mr. Bird, the phys. ed. teacher. He had written "Don't" in big, bold letters on the board, asked if there were any questions and then let them practice jump shots on the basketball court. It was a neat class. In any event, they concluded computers were far more interesting than girls, and decided to pursue the former, at least for now.

For several years Jeff had asked his parents for a computer, but to no avail. Willard's dad had gone into a fit of laughter when Willard suggested that a computer would probably help him get better grades. Their only option, if they were going to get near a computer anytime soon, was to enroll in Mr. Bird's computer course. And from day one, they knew they had found their intellectual home.

The computers were new to the school that year and the cause of much scrambling and extra work for a number of people. They were set up temporarily in a regular classroom because there was no budget for major renovations to the building. Cables and power cords were simply bundled and run between the rows of desks, and several printers were grouped together near the newly installed modem line at the far end of the room.

Mr. Bird, the phys. ed. teacher, was given all of the manuals that came with the computers to read and digest before the lab could open. There was a sizable pile on his desk: the system manual, the network manual, the printer manual, the master reference manual, the modem manual, and the instructions that came with all of the software.

Mr. Scrivner had a degree in computer science and would gladly have helped Mr. Bird master all of that reading, but he was too busy taking over several of Mr. Bird's phys. ed. classes. The principal was an odd duck who believed that if you had a specialty, it's best not to let you teach it, because you will probably want to run things your way and not "our way," by which he meant "his way." He said that both Mr. Bird and Mr. Scrivner would someday thank him for making it possible for each of them to expand their areas of expertise through cross-disciplinary teaching. And he said it with a straight face, too. However, as the new term began and both Bird and Scrivner struggled with their new assignments, gratitude was not an emotion either of them experienced often.

The computer lab was a zoo. Even if Mr. Bird had intended to read all those manuals, it was beyond the ability of any normal man to master them all, and he didn't. Jeff did. He loved the manuals. He thought they were sexy. Willard liked the illustrations. If you just read the pictures, you could make the computers do almost anything they were designed to do. Most of the kids quickly learned a little elementary word processing, and some went on to experiment with poster writing and cartooning with clip art. Jeff and Willard were into graphic design and game programming and hanging out with geeks in other schools who could also get access to modems and computer time or had their own systems.

Jeff knew there was a vast array of computer networks out there just waiting for a pair of enterprising hackers to contact and explore. Mr. Bird, however, had a most annoying habit of checking up on his students and requiring that they complete the assigned work to pass the course. That really reduced the class time Jeff and Willard had for self-expression. It was Willard who solved the problem. When Mr. Bird was sick for a few days, the sub who came in to cover his classes would pick up the key to the computer lab from the office in the morning and drop it off again at night before walking back the entire length of the school to get to her car in the parking lot. Willard simply offered to drop the key off for the sub after the last class one day and then went looking for a key-cutting machine to get a duplicate made. He was a bit worried about handing the key in to the office in the morning, but he told the secretary he just forgot to hand it in the night before. Knowing Willard, she never suspected anything was amiss.

Getting into the building was a bit of a problem, but they found a ground-floor window with a latch that could be slipped with a long, flexible shim they had made in Shop. Once inside, they closed and locked the window, knowing that when they entered the hall, the classroom door would automatically lock behind them. The lab was on the second floor, and the key worked perfectly. When they were ready to leave, they left by the back exit from the school as they usually did each night, and the door closed and locked behind them. From that fateful day on, they never missed a weekend date with the computers, and with the blackout drapes closed, no one ever suspected they were there.

Their first adventures were pretty standard. Jeff read the manuals and tended to interrupt Willard's game programming with cries of excited discovery. Jeff's special interest was the modem. The school did have a dedicated computer line, but no high-speed connection to a service provider for easy access to the Internet. There was talk of dial-up service for the individual schools, but the cost would have been significant and, besides, no one in the educational system had any idea what the schools could use Internet access for anyway. The modems they did have were intended only to allow teachers in the individual schools to update student marks on a weekly basis by connecting directly to the county's educational administration office.

Willard lost interest in programming for a while when Jeff made contact with the county's library computer. It was incredibly easy. He got the number of the computer line and the password by simply checking out the list taped to the secretary's desk when he asked to use the phone after school one day. The next Sunday they dialled into the library system and excitedly wandered about in the bowels of the software that controlled all the circulation, purchasing and applications files needed to run the large library system. When Jeff and Willard discovered how to access the files for their own school, they were in awe of their new-found power. Their little hearts raced as they checked out who was on the overdue list, who was waiting for what books and what new arrivals could be expected to show up on the library shelves soon.

Their first tentative venture into the workings of the library computer was very nearly their last. Willard suggested they enhance the reading material in the libraries of the county's schools by ordering Playboy, as he was still hankering after a better understanding of the opposite sex. Jeff didn't like the sound of the name, and suggested Playgirl instead, not knowing if such a magazine existed but assuming that it must, since it was a far more interesting title. Jeff won and Willard was happy, but the head librarian was royally ticked off to discover the addition to the purchasing suggestions stored in the acquisitions file.

Jeff and Willard were the immediate suspects for the prank for several reasons. First, while neither had shown either aptitude or interest in any scholastic activity more complicated than fingerpainting, they were both totally absorbed by the computers, and with the modem in particular. Second, they could run circles around Mr. Bird in computer class and they enjoyed a kind of celebrity status with the other kids based on their intuitive grasp of how the computers worked and their willingness to distribute copies of the computer games they had written or downloaded from local bulletin boards. And lastly, the stunt was so dumb it had Jeff and Willard written all over it. But since Mr. Bird assured the district supervisor that no one had used the school's modem in class over the last week, and because he was sure that neither Jeff nor Willard had a home system that could access the county's library computer, they were off the hook. However, the flak from that initial blunder cost them several sleepless nights.

Sleepless nights notwithstanding, they soon moved on to establish contact with other hackers, and once again their world expanded. After the near-disaster with the library computer, they were initially very cautious about what information they shared and what questions they asked of the other geeks they met through local bulletin boards. There were a number of local dial-up or point-to-point bulletin boards not connected to the Internet that they could access directly, and some of them catered to highly technical computer questions. They called themselves Spock and Kirk and were surprised at how quickly they were accepted and how easily they fit into the hacker community. The whole point of the contacts was information sharing, and their skills expanded with each new session.

But Jeff still wanted access to the Internet, and Willard got so sick of listening to him gripe about it that he called up a local service provider and tried to make an application over the phone for service on the school's computer line. He mentioned it casually to Jeff the next day when they were eating lunch in the cafeteria, and Jeff nearly choked on his sandwich. He stopped breathing and was turning bright red, but Willard didn't notice and continued on with his narrative until he reached the part where the service rep had hung up on him. The rep had pressed Willard for the phone number of the line he wanted service on, and when Willard said he couldn't remember the number or the billing address, the rep said Willard should call back when he was ready to get serious and hung up. Jeff managed to get the bite down and when he could breathe again, he told Willard that the guidance counsellor had been correct when she described Willard as "somewhat socially inept," but Willard couldn't see what that had to do with anything.

Nevertheless, by the end of that lunch hour, they both realized that, because of the risk of someone finding out about their illegal use of the computer lab, conventional Internet access was not an option. So they went looking for an unconventional solution to the access problem, and it didn't take long to find one. They called up a geek they knew and put their problem to him. He was a guy they had met through a bulletin board; he bought used computers and upgraded and resold them out of a small electronics shop in town. He said he understood their problem and he thought he had something that would do the job. After school the next day, they dropped into his shop; he showed them a program called Snoop and Scoop, a program he had written to hack into systems over the Internet.

To use his program, he said the target system had to be up and running and have access to a server. If it was, he could enter it and snoop to his heart's content, even if the owner was using the machine at the same time. But Snoop and Scoop had a second function that would probably be of more interest to them. It could also mask your own phone number while you were hacking into a system. Say you wanted to hack into a software company to get a pre-release copy of a new game, and their geeks were sharp enough to know they had been hacked and ticked off enough to come looking for you. If you knew the phone number of a system with dial-up Internet access, Snoop and Scoop could dial into that system, provided it was up and running but not already online, and scan its hard drive for the phone number of its server and its access password. Snoop and Scoop could then call out to the system's server, using its password, and the server would think the call was coming from its customer and, theoretically at least, no trace would be possible past the customer's number. Of course, if the owner was sitting at his computer, he might wonder why his modem was squealing, so you had to be careful when you used it. But once on the Internet, you could go anywhere you wanted to, anonymously and for free. And to Jeff and Willard that sounded a lot like a solution to their access problem. They left with a copy of Snoop and Scoop and couldn't wait for Sunday to try it out for themselves.

Snoop and Scoop was awesome! They gained access to the county's municipal computer late one night and checked out the names of the newly dead in the city morgue from the public information file that would be sent to the newspaper the next morning. That was so spooky, they stopped for a double-cheese pizza on the way home from the computer lab. They decided that they should be able to do something even more interesting than just read the names of the newly departed and then go home. The next Sunday they checked to see what flights were arriving and departing from the local airport. They could have got the same information from TV via the local cable network channel, but it was more fun to locate and access it via a hack into the computer supplying that information to the cable company. They began rummaging about in the school's computer files at the county office. They never changed their report-card marks, but they occasionally downloaded advance copies of math and accounting tests, together with the answers thoughtfully supplied by the teachers who had written them, eventually proving that Willard's remark to his father had been prophetic: having computer access did help them improve their marks.

They tested Snoop and Scoop for several weeks. It worked perfectly, and with each successful hack, their confidence grew. They peeked into various systems and poked around in different files, as voyeurs might stand about gawking into other people's living-room windows. They weren't malicious. They never erased data or ordered things using other people's credit card accounts. But they did pick up some useful information that the systems' owners thought was private and totally secure. It was time, Jeff suggested, to take it to the Internet.

Their next adventure was their first real hack. Jeff had checked the phone book for fax numbers to local businesses, guessing correctly that the fax machine and the computer shared the same line in many small offices and that a simple switching device would direct incoming calls according to the signal received. The phone line was always open, so if the computer was up and running, Snoop and Scoop could access it easily. And more importantly, Denton City was a local call from the county just a few miles away, and there would be no long-distance charges to show up on the school's computer line and alert the office to what they were doing.

A travel agent in Denton City had left her computer up and running over the weekend, and Jeff found her password for the reservations system at Pelican Airlines International stored in a data file on her hard drive. This was a perfect launch pad to the Internet. On a Sunday early in November, they connected with Pelican Airlines' reservation system using the password and identification code of the travel agent they had hacked. All they wanted to do was read the names of people booked on Pelican Airlines flights for Christmas vacations. They accessed the roster of Pelican Airlines International, Flight 038 to Paris, France, departing Gate C at 9:45 a.m., December 24, and the rest of the cryptic details about the ETA and the route. Imagine their surprise when Mr. Scrivner's name came up. It was their Mr. Scrivner. They knew his address and phone number from the teachers' information file on the county's system. And they looked in wonder at the flashing cursor, obligingly asking if they wanted to change the reservation or leave it confirmed.

They couldn't resist. They checked other flights leaving the same day from the same gate at about the same time, and there was one for Brussels. They booked him onto that one, then watched in fascination as the information necessary to confirm a reservation on one flight and destination was changed to another. Suddenly frightened, they selected the Change option a second time and keyed in the original information, wisely recorded by Jeff. They were greatly relieved when they saw the original information reappear as if by magic. They were not into creating chaos, and it jolted them to think how much damage they could have caused by just fooling around. They shut the system down quickly, before the genie could escape from his bottle again and create a disaster from which they might not be able to recover.

On Sunday, November 14, they selected Denton City's computer system, thinking it would be a more challenging hack and far less likely to get them into trouble. It was a big, old mainframe and every City department stored its data on it, both public information and confidential files. They were using the travel agent's system again, even though Jeff was uneasy about it. There was something about going through the same access route too often that bothered him, but when they couldn't find another system up and running, they drifted back to the one system that always seemed to be available. Initially they were denied access, and Willard, easily bored, bailed out to go work on one of his action games. Jeff kept tinkering. Snoop and Scoop had an access feature he had never tried—Password Bypass. It was complicated and it took him a while to figure out, but it worked. The computer screen went blank, then switched to snow, and eventually flashed "I'm thinking" before going blank again. Then Denton City's logo appeared on the screen.

"We're in," Jeff yelled.

Willard came quickly from his own computer to Jeff's to stare at the logo on the screen. After a moment he said, "It's flat."

"What?" Jeff asked, turning to look at Willard over his shoulder.

"The logo," said Willard, pointing to the image on the screen. "It's flat. Like they just took a picture of a sign and scanned it in. It just sits there. I thought it would be animated. You know, like a flag waving in the wind or something."

"Not everything has to blow up, Willard," said Jeff. "Maybe they like it flat. Or maybe they just don't care. But is that all you can say: 'It's flat'?"

"Well, it is flat. What am I supposed to say?"

"How about, 'Great hack, Jeff! Way to go!' Or something like that, eh? I always tell you it's great when you do something far-out."

"Okay. Great-hack-Jeff-way-to-go," he said as he ambled back to sit at his usual work station and yawned, indicating he had lost interest in programming for that evening.

"You're hopeless, Willard. Is there any pizza left?"

"No," said Willard, pretending to peer into the box as he licked his fingers, wiping them absently on his pants. "But you can have the cheese off the lid, and there's a bunch of olives in the box." Willard hated olives. Jeff settled for another can of Coke and busied himself with his keyboard. After a few minutes Willard asked, "What are you doing now?"

Jeff was deep into the data files and slowly reading the menu for files in the tax department. "Tax files," he said. "I want to see how they organize data."

"Why?" Willard asked.

"I just think this stuff is interesting," said Jeff. "This is the file of the taxes everybody pays on their houses and offices and stuff, and it looks like a stand-alone file. It should be linked with all their other data files, but it doesn't seem like it is."

"What's wrong with having a stand-alone file for important stuff?" said Willard. "That way, an error in one file won't corrupt the data in all the other files."

Jeff said nothing for a while and continued to scroll down the tax records. Willard stretched and got up to wander around for a few minutes, eventually coming back to peer over Jeff's shoulder. Jeff slowed the data and advanced one record at a time and then stopped.

"Hey. That's our house," said Willard, now fully engrossed in the data showing on the screen. "Does it say how much our taxes are?"

Jeff pointed to the extreme right of the record and Willard read the figure out loud.

"Seems to operate the same as the flight reservations system at Pelican," Jeff said. "There's a Change Data option in a utility menu that you can turn off if you're just searching data. The field names are posted here along the top and a window rolls records up to them as you scroll down the page."

"Bring up your house," Willard said. Jeff scrolled down until he found it, and they spent a few minutes looking at that data. Then Willard said, "Let me run it for a minute."

Jeff rolled off to the side and Willard pulled up to the keyboard. "What's the command for Search?" he asked, and Jeff told him how to bring up the utility menu.

Willard typed "Scrivner, Winston, T." into the Search function and instantly the record was displayed. "He owns a condo, so that must be the apartment number after the street address. And he has a mortgage for $109,000; wow, that's a lot. And his taxes are paid for the whole year."

Willard sat looking at the record for almost a minute. He already had the utility menu on the screen and Scrivner's was the only record displayed. He scrolled up the menu and hit the Change Data option. The Search function disappeared and was replaced with the Change Data function.

"Willard, we shouldn't mess with anything yet until we know the system," Jeff said.

Willard moved the cursor to the column headed Taxes Paid and looked at the Y in Scrivner's record. "Wouldn't it be neat," he said, "if Mr. Scrivner got another bill for his taxes when they're already paid? Being an accounting teacher, I bet he'd go bananas." He shifted the cursor to the Overdue column.

Jeff leaned over and took hold of Willard's arm. "Don't mess with it, Willard. We don't know the system, and it could be a problem. Let's just leave it be, okay?"

The blinking cursor was already positioned in the Overdue column and Willard simply typed Y and pressed the enter key. Instantly the Y replaced the N, which had been showing in the Overdue column, and N replaced the Y, which had been showing in the Taxes Paid column.

Jeff yelled "No!" but it was too late. The screen went blank even as he spoke.

Willard turned to Jeff and shrugged. "It'll be in memory. It won't be gone. I'll just flip the Overdue column with the Taxes Paid column and things will be back like they were."

Then Scrivner's data was gone and the utility menu was alone on the screen with a new line reading Reason for Change, followed by a single box in which the blinking cursor now sat. Jeff was wringing his hands and making little gurgling sounds that didn't stop even when he ran out of breath. Willard had a puzzled look on his face, like he didn't understand what the computer was asking. When he tried to scroll up to find the Change Data function, the cursor was unresponsive, still blinking in the single lighted box.

"There has to be an override command," Jeff finally said. "Let's try to escape out of this screen," knowing it was hopeless even as he elbowed Willard out of the way and punched the escape key. The screen cleared. They held their breath, and then it displayed Incomplete Procedure: Reason for Change Must Be Stated, and took them back to the line reading, Reason for Change, with its little box and the cursor stubbornly blinking in it. Jeff started gurgling again. Willard had to go for a pee.

When Willard returned, Jeff was still banging away, trying to override the utility menu to get back to the data screen, but they both knew it wasn't going to happen. Willard said, "It wants a letter or a number from zero to nine in the box. So, like, we have one chance out of thirty-six to hit the right key."

Jeff looked up, confused, then turned to Willard and in a high, squeaky voice asked, "What? What are you talking about?"

"The box," said Willard. "It's only big enough for one digit or one letter, so twenty-six letters and ten numbers. Thirty-six choices."

Jeff nodded slowly, considering what Willard was saying. "Right," he said, "you're right. It wants a single-digit command. But we don't know what any of the commands will do." Then, looking hard at Willard, he added, "And I'm pretty sure there isn't any command that says, 'Willard was just messing around, and we would like to get the original data back please!' You've really done it this time, Willard. If Mr. Scrivner doesn't kill us for messing up his taxes, Mr. Bird will for messing with the computers or Mr. Burden will just because we were stupid!"

"Okay," said Willard. "How about we just shut the machine off and go home? It's late and I'm hungry."

Jeff shook his head and said, "No! No, we can't just shut it down. If we do, it will just loop inside itself and the tax people will have to ask the programmers to break the loop, and then the city guys will know they've been hacked and then they'll be looking for us, too! No. We don't have a choice. We have to answer its questions and exit the program through Snoop and Scoop and let the tax people find the error we made and fix it themselves. Or if they don't find it, maybe Mr. Scrivner will just get another tax bill or something. But he's all paid up and he'll have a receipt or bank statement or something to say it's paid. They can't make him pay it again, can they? So that's it. That's what we have to do."

Jeff sounded a good deal more confident than he obviously felt, because he rolled his chair back to make room for Willard.

Willard just said, "Okay", rolled up to the keyboard and started punching in numbers with one finger. He gave it a zero and pressed the enter key. Nothing happened. The zero didn't appear and the cursor remained blinking in the empty box. He entered each number in sequence with the same result. The computer would not recognize a numerical input. He started into the letters and had no better luck until he hit D. When he pressed the enter key, the screen cleared and they thought they were home free, but after a few seconds the screen produced eight boxes for them to fill in, labelled Year, Month and Day.

Jeff jerked upright and asked in a panic, "What date? Why does it want a date?"

Willard shrugged impassively, as he always did when he got hungry and bored, and said, "The date of the latest change, I guess. What's the date today?"

"No!" Jeff yelled, excitedly pulling Willard back from the keyboard. "We can't give it today's date, because it's Sunday and they can't know that's when we changed the data." Calmer now, he said, "I'll give it Friday's date and they'll think they made the mistake." And he did, but the computer wouldn't take it.

Willard stood and started gathering up all their stuff. "Just type in dates until it accepts one. I want to go."

Jeff hesitated for a moment, then he filled in the blanks with suitable numbers, hoping the input would be accepted. There was a second or two pause, but the input was rejected. He tried several more times, offering the computer earlier dates each time. He did not record the last date he gave it, some three months earlier in the year, but for some reason the computer was happy with it. Suddenly the screen cleared and the utility menu reappeared, asking if they wished to make any more changes. He was so desperate to get out of the loop that he instinctively entered No and was instantly back to the main menu.

Willard had shut his machine down and was standing at the door ready to leave. Jeff looked up at him and nodded Okay. He knew they should go back into the file and reverse the changes they had made, but he was afraid of getting into yet another interminable loop, and he couldn't face that again. He said, "Just let me back out. It'll only take a minute."

Slowly he keyed in the command to bring up Snoop and Scoop and then punched in the complicated commands to exit the program. By the time he had finished, Willard had already left the room and was waiting for him at the back exit.

They shared a feeling of dread as they headed back to Mr. Pizza, and not even extra cheese on a meat-lover's special made it go away. Willard's only comment on the fiasco was that he didn't think it was too bad, but Jeff wasn't sure if Willard was talking about the computer mess or the spot of pizza goo he was trying to wipe off his best T-shirt. In fact, they both knew it was bad. They had screwed up big-time, but neither of them had a clue what to do about it or how bad it was really going to get.

Monday came and went and the sky didn't fall on them. So when Tuesday and Wednesday and the rest of the week passed uneventfully, they began to hope that maybe things were going to be all right after all.

But things were not going to be all right. In fact things had not been all right for any number of people at City Hall during that whole, long, miserable week. The accounting department discovered the imbalance in the property tax file when they booted the system on Monday morning, but the accountants hadn't a clue where the error had come from. The clerks responsible for inputting data into those files were immediately defensive, and one of them said what they were all thinking: "You just know they will blame us for this mess." An error-checking search was begun immediately, a joint effort between the accountants and the data-entry clerks, but it was very slow going. It rapidly degenerated into a finger-pointing exercise, and by coffee time they weren't talking to each other. By lunchtime the chief accountant was thinking of taking up smoking again, and the department was running out of Post-It notes.

Things improved somewhat after the office manager circulated a note requiring that all messages on Post-It notes be date and time stamped and signed, but the memo about sticking a vulgar message in the middle of someone's screen being actionable as a union grievance seemed to calm things down considerably. Meanwhile, Eric Sorensen, the city's programmer, and his department took no part in the chicken fight over who had entered what bad data into what file. Rather, they assumed they had yet another previously undetected bug in their program and set about debugging every line of code in the entire system again. They knew nothing about the illegal entry into their computer, but they knew something smelled very fishy and they had to find out what it was.

Of course, Jeff and Willard were totally unaware of the havoc they'd created and, by the beginning of the second week, they had just about convinced themselves that there would be no fallout from their latest blunder. Then came Tuesday, November the twenty-third, and that's when Mr. Scrivner started acting really strange.

He didn't get to school until after 9:00 Tuesday morning and was more sour than usual, because he was too late to get breakfast.

He told his class as much and added that his alarm hadn't gone off because the power was out in his condo. After lunch Willard was in the office and heard him on the phone with the city's electrical authority, asking when the power would be back on in his neighbourhood. Apparently it was not a problem with the neighbourhood, just his condo. Then he called the manager of his condo complex, but Willard had to return to class and couldn't hear the rest of the conversation.

By Wednesday morning things were getting really weird. Scrivner arrived at school with Mr. Bird, and Jeff overheard Mr. Bird telling Miss Wilmore that Scrivner had stayed with him Tuesday night, because the city had turned the power off in Scrivner's condo and he couldn't get them to turn it back on. And as if that wasn't bad enough, Scrivner said someone from the city had also changed the locks on his doors and he couldn't even get into his own apartment. No warning, no explanation, no nothing!

Then the secretary told the janitor that Mr. Scrivner must be in big financial trouble, because his bank account was frozen and the county couldn't even deposit his cheque into his account. And she had heard him talking to the manager of his condo and there was apparently some problem with the city over his utility bills. She warned the janitor not to tell a soul, but telling him anything was like putting up a notice on the bulletin board, and soon Scrivner's problems were the only topic of conversation for staff and students alike.

Then, around 3:30 on Thursday afternoon, a tow truck arrived at school and towed Scrivner's car away. For a few minutes, it looked like Scrivner and the tow truck driver might have a punch-up over the car, but the driver threatened to call the police to enforce the towing order he had and in the end he just hooked the car up and drove off with it. The driver didn't want to talk to Scrivner anymore, so he left the letter he had brought for him at the office, and Scrivner got it when he came down to hand in his attendance records for the day. He read it quickly and then barged into an empty office to call somebody and slammed the door. The cleaning lady, the janitor's wife who worked part-time cleaning the front offices, couldn't hear the conversation. But Scrivner stormed out, forgetting the letter on the desk, and she read it before replacing it in his box. It was better than the soaps, she thought. The letter was from the finance company to explain why they had seized his car. It said the bank had not processed the usual monthly deduction from his account to the finance company, and they had taken pre-emptive action to seize the car because of the unusual financial problems created when a bank account is frozen. They explained that the only security the finance company has on its automobile loans is the car itself, and the manager figured a frozen bank account was reason enough to move fast and sort things out after they had control of the car. But Mr. Scrivner could have his car back as soon as he brought his payments up to date.

Scrivner went to the gym office to wait for Mr. Bird and used the phone in the office to call his bank manager to find out why the November payment had not been made on his car and what was this nonsense about his account being frozen. The manager said that yes, apparently the account had been frozen by their regional office earlier in the week and there was no point in yelling at him about it. Once an account is frozen, no money can be transferred into or out of the account until that order is reversed. However, he did say that with the bank's expanded hours of service, Mr. Scrivner could come down until six that evening and talk to the staff about his problem. Of course, the accounts manager was the person he should talk to, but she was sick today and probably wouldn't be in tomorrow, either. But if he wanted to come in on Monday, somebody would probably be able to help him. Scrivner told him what he could do with his extended hours and slammed the phone down. Only then did he look up to see the shocked faces of the students who were putting equipment away in the storage area on the other side of the window in the gym office. He was trying to remember just how salty his comment to the banker had been as he followed Mr. Bird out to his car.

It was a little before five that evening when they got back to Bill Bird's apartment, so Scrivner called the city's electrical services again to find out why they had cut the power to his unit. But the clerk remembered him from his earlier call and wouldn't talk to him. He'd been really snarky with her, and she told him to contact the city's Department of Administrative Services, because she had no new information to give him and disconnected. Since Scrivner had no other leads to follow up, he called.

Scrivner waited the obligatory three rings until someone picked up the direct line to the administration department, and a pleasant voice said, "Hello. You have reached Denton City's Department of Administrative Services."

"Hi," said Scrivner, "My name is..." But that was as far as he got.

"Please listen to the following five options before making your selection," the voice continued, ignoring with regal disdain his ill-advised attempt to derail its program.

"For information regarding a late billing date or for municipal services, please press..." It droned on, intent on listing all five options, but Scrivner was too wound up to wait. He hit zero, hoping to get the receptionist, but the wretched little system was waiting for him and took him back to the beginning of its candy-sweet, mechanical monologue, starting at "Please listen..." A very subtle, but extremely astute, put-down. When it reached the fifth option he screamed loud enough for Bill to check from the living room to see what was happening. He moved quickly to prevent Scrivner from doing something quite drastic with the receiver. The mechanical voice was purring, "For all other general inquires please press zero. Thank you and have a nice day."

Scrivner composed himself, took the receiver from Bill and, with deadly calm, pressed zero, which the system now accepted, presumably because it deemed he had been properly chastised for his earlier rash behaviour.

After the additional obligatory three rings, the phone was answered by a clerk who identified himself as Mr. Hefflendorf.

Even as Hefflendorf pronounced his name, Scrivner knew he was doomed. The squeaky little voice, reed-thin and projecting a tone that fluctuated between hopelessness and complete despair, asked in apparent sincerity, "How can I help you, sir?"

Scrivner took a deep breath and began. He identified himself, and Mr. Hefflendorf said, "Yes." He explained he was a property owner and gave the address of his condo, to which Mr. Hefflendorf replied, "Yes." He launched into his story, determined to finish it before Hefflendorf could interrupt again, but he ran out of breath and paused just long enough for Hefflendorf to get in another "Yes." Scrivner could hear the resignation in the tone of the man's voice, as though each statement he made was driving the little man ever closer to throwing himself under the wheels of the first passing bus. At Scrivner's request, Mr. Hefflendorf put his file up on the screen and was now confirming the painful details aloud as Scrivner took him through the whole sorry tale.

"Look," said Scrivner, "all I want is for you to tell the electrical department to please turn the power on again in my apartment and to find out who changed the locks and to give me the keys. I have never in my life been late with a utility payment, so I have no idea why they shut the power off in the first place. Oh, and for that matter, I would like to know why the locks were changed. No one seems to know in your electrical department, and I am getting the runaround from the maintenance department too. At least I think it was the maintenance department who changed the locks on my place. Anyway, what about it? Can we get this mess cleared up?"

"Well," said Hefflendorf, "we are showing a TS code under your electrical billing file. That's the code that would have triggered the work order to terminate your electric service. And we are also showing a PD code in your billing file. That's our code to indicate your electric bill has been paid up to date. My goodness, that is strange."

Scrivner stepped into the pause and said, "Good, good. So you do have confirmation that the power has been turned off in my apartment and that I am not behind in my payments. Well, that's certainly progress. Now, can you please issue the order to reverse it?"

"Er, well," said Hefflendorf. "Um, it's not quite that simple. You see, while that would normally be enough to reverse the order, er…having both a PD code and a TS code in the same account, there is still the problem of the changed locks. You see, it's city policy that the electrical department cannot turn the power on again until the apartment is unsealed."

"Unsealed? It's not sealed," Scrivner said. "Some bonehead just changed the locks, that's all!"

"Yes, er, well, you see," said Hefflendorf, the resignation in his voice now betraying that he knew this problem would never be resolved, "Er, we also have an SP code. That's our code for 'seal the premises' and that code would have to be reversed before we could reverse the TS code and issue a BS code for 'begin service.'"

"Well, then, just do it! What's the problem? You people put it on and you can jolly well take it off, and the sooner the better. Doesn't that make perfect sense to you, Heffendorf?"

"That's 'Hefflendorf,' sir, with an 'l,' and please don't shout at me. I know you're upset, but…" He paused and Scrivner could hear him gulping something—probably water and some antacid tablets. He sounded like a man with stomach problems.

After a moment he came back on the line and excused himself before going on, "As I was saying, I know you're upset, sir, but there's no reason to take it out on me. I'm just answering your questions as best I can and I'm getting a headache."

He was almost whining now and Scrivner knew he had to back off or he would lose whatever help this little man could offer him. "Of course you're right, Mr., er, Hefflendorf, and I do apologize. I got carried away. I'm a teacher and we are in the middle of exams and mine are all locked up in my apartment and I can't even get them to finish marking them. And I am staying with a friend because I can't get into my own apartment and no one seems to know why I am locked out since all my utility payments are up to date! Sorry. I'm sorry. I know I was getting carried away again. So, er…so what can you tell me about the locks being changed?"

"Well, yes, the locks were changed, as I said, pursuant to an SP order. That order would have been issued automatically by the computer. Let me just change screens and…find…the comments. Yes, here we are. The city does not have a security deposit to cover the utility bills in the event you move out without paying your bill, and that explains it," he said, more confident now that he had some hard data to quote.

"What!" said Scrivner, before he could catch himself. By now he was in no mood to pander to this wimp, who seemed to have some influence but not the backbone to use it. "Since when did the City require a security deposit on the electrical account? I've lived there for five years and I never had to have one before. What's this all about?"

"Er, well, er," Hefflendorf sputtered before just stopping altogether. After a very long moment, he continued in an oddly rushed manner. "If you own the apartment, you don't need a security deposit, but if you are just renting, well then you do. Do you know who was living in your apartment for the last three months?"

"Living in my apartment for the last three months?" bellowed Scrivner. "Well, me of course? Who would you think was there?" Then in a more conciliatory tone he asked, "Why? What does your record say about who was living there?"

Hefflendorf was positively shaking now; Scrivner could hear it in his voice. "Well, er," his voice died again. "Well, that is…"

Scrivner bellowed, "Well, tell me what else it says!"

"Um…er…well…" He took a deep breath and then said in a rush, "It says you have not paid your taxes for the last year and that you died on August tenth of this year. So, you haven't been living in the apartment and whoever is living there has not put down a security deposit and that's why the SP order was issued." There was urgency to his tone and he was rushing even faster to get it all out. "Your file does not list any next of kin in the city, so when you were reported deceased as of August 10, the computer would have informed the legal department so they could prepare a final statement of moneys owing to the city and file the proper documents to lay a claim against the estate, especially since you had not paid your taxes for an entire year. And because someone else was obviously living in your apartment, as indicated by the continuing utility bills, but the city had not received the required security deposit, the maintenance department would have been informed to secure the premises, pending probate of your estate. Now if you will excuse me, I am not feeling well at all. This is giving me an awful headache, and my stomach is acting up as well."

"Haven't paid my t..." Scrivner stopped mid-bellow. He was going to ream the little man out over the taxes, but that bit about having died three months ago stopped him cold. "Now wait a minute. That's got to be a computer error. This whole thing is a silly mistake. Somebody screwed up and you have an error in your data file. You just need to correct the error," he said in a far more conciliatory tone then he had started with.

"That's not possible, sir. We have never had a data error. The computer is checked every day and I assure you if there was an error we would have found it and corrected it. And besides we don't have any error-correcting procedure as far as I know, and I would know because...because I just would, that's all!"

The worm had turned and Scrivner was now facing a Hefflendorf with his back up, but also, alas, with his gimpy tummy and a nasty headache. Scrivner knew he was not going to hang in there much longer, so he tried a different tack.

"Mr. Hefflendorf, would it surprise you if I told you that bit about having died three months ago is news to me? As a matter of fact, I feel quite good at the moment and very much alive. And I would really appreciate it if you would just get a little memo off to your data people to ask them to please find their little error and fix it for me. What do you say, Mr. H.? Will you do that for me, hmm? Please?"

"I'm sorry, sir. I'm not allowed to spend more than five minutes with any one caller and you've been on this line for six minutes already. And as I said, I really don't feel very well."

"This is getting really silly, Hefflendorf!" Scrivner said, in what he hoped was an authoritative voice. But that was as far as he got. That same candy-sweet, mechanical voice cut him off with a cheery, "Thank you for calling Denton City's Department of Administrative Services. All our offices are now closed. If you would like a listing of our hours of operation, please call...."

Over dinner Scrivner explained what he had learned to Bill Bird and as he explained it he began to see that in a crazy sort of way it did make some sense. The city had filed the claim against his estate to collect the taxes they thought he owed, because their computer had said he was dead. The bank held the mortgage on his property and had first claim to it after the taxes were paid. So the city's legal department would have faxed the bank a notice about the claim they were filing because of the bank's interest in the property. And the bank, having been officially informed of a civil action involving the estate of the late Winston T. Scrivner, would have frozen his accounts and cancelled his credit card. And since the big lenders all share credit information among themselves, it was a good bet that his other credit cards were cancelled as well.

It was obviously some stupid computer error, but until it was cleared up nobody was going to talk to him, not the bank or the finance company or anybody else.

Later that evening, after Bill had gone off to a meeting, Scrivner sat glumly, stirring his coffee, trying to assure himself that bad as it was, it could have been worse. He could stay with Bill for a few more days. Bill had loaned him a set of sweats and Scrivner had picked up some shirts and stuff because all the rest of his clothes were locked in his apartment. It was the end of November and the kids were still writing exams, so he didn't have classes to prepare for in the morning. However, all of the exams he had already marked and the report-card marks he needed to hand into the office by Monday were locked up in the apartment. The rest of the exams were being written tomorrow. But he would not be in school tomorrow. He would have to take Friday off to go down and see the city and whoever else to get this mess cleared up. Surely, he thought, it wouldn't take more than a day.... No sooner had he formed the thought than he realized that he could not unscramble this mess in just one day. He would probably die of old age before they finally admitted that he wasn't already dead!

Bill could pick up Scrivner's last set of exams on Friday and Scrivner could mark them over the weekend. He knew his term marks were up to date but his mark book was somewhere in his filing cabinet in the computer lab, and he wondered if Bill could find it. With his term marks and the exam marks, Scrivner could at least calculate the report-card marks for some of his classes by Monday. It would have been simpler to work at school on Saturday or Sunday, but with the new security system being tested over the weekend there was no way he would be able to get into his classroom until Monday. There would be no marks for most of his classes to turn in by Monday, and the principal was going to skin him alive. Some days, he thought, it just wasn't worth getting out of bed.

On the plus side, he had picked up the travellers' cheques for his Christmas trip and, by sheer good luck, had not left them in his apartment. With his driver's licence as identification, he could cash those in any store in the city. The very thought of the Christmas holiday he had booked and paid for started him wondering if his passport would also have been revoked or cancelled or whatever they do with your passport when you're dead. He just couldn't face any more bad news at the moment. But there was more bad news to come. He was absolutely sure of that even as he pulled out the phone book to look up the principal's home number.

The first priority was to get some time off, starting tomorrow. There was no point in talking to the bank or anybody else until the city corrected its error and reversed the legal actions that had created the problem in the first place, and he would have to see them in person. That meant calling Mr. Burden, the principal, at home tonight to explain that he needed a few days off because he couldn't deal with the city over the phone. He dreaded making the call. Burden was in a perpetual bad mood even on his good days. He would not be sympathetic and he didn't even know the meaning of the word "helpful."

When Scrivner called to ask for a leave, pleading a personal emergency, Burden ignored his request and reminded him that he had not yet handed in any marks to the office. Scrivner tried to fudge it, but Burden forced him to admit that he no longer had the exams he had already marked and that he did not know when he could turn in his marks. Burden said that was unacceptable and that if Scrivner did not show up for work Friday he could consider himself on suspension until Burden met with the superintendent to review what further disciplinary measures would be taken, and then he hung up.

Well, that was that. Scrivner contemplated the irony of his situation. Since he was suspended, he had the time off that he needed to get this mess all straightened out. So when it was cleared up and everybody knew he was not really dead, he would be able to collect unemployment insurance in his own name! Winston T. Scrivner was not a happy man and, though he did not know it and would have found no comfort in the fact if he had known it, he was not alone. There were a lot of unhappy people in Denton City this Thursday evening.

The city's programming department had suffered a rude awakening when all this mess had started nearly two weeks earlier. An error in the numbers from the tax department had been flagged by the internal security program. The numbers always had to balance at the end of each day, and though they had balanced on the Friday evening, they did not balance when they booted the system the following Monday morning. It took several days of going over the files, but by Friday afternoon of that first week the clerks in the tax department had found the error. According to the computer files, one taxpayer, Mr. Winston T. Scrivner, had paid his taxes in full and even had a small credit in his property tax account. Yet this same Mr. Scrivner was listed on the tax roll as owing over a year's taxes and in fact had been dead even before he made his last payment. Interesting. Once the tax department had found the error, Eric Sorensen and his staff could start tracking the error back to its source, and that proved remarkably easy.

The system had an entry log and it showed the change to Scrivner's file had been made on Sunday evening, but none of the managers who had the password for the tax files had logged onto the system over the weekend. Their system had been entered illegally: they had been hacked. The passwords had been bypassed. It had probably been a simple brute-force attack using a random character generator to tease out each letter until the hacker found the right combination to gain entry into the system. They knew when the changes had been made but, thanks to Snoop and Scoop, no direct evidence of the illegal entry was left behind in the computer for the programmers to find. But there was a record, and once they realized that they had been hacked, they knew exactly where that record was stored.

To prevent unauthorized long-distance calling by city employees, all phone lines in the city hall complex, including the computer lines, were monitored, and each call entering or leaving the complex was logged by date, time and phone number. This was a service instituted years earlier, provided by the phone company and recorded on its equipment in a data centre not connected directly to the city's mainframe. Since the hack was traced to the weekend, it would not take long to isolate calls made to the system over the weekend, and Sorensen would request that a search be made as soon as the data centre opened on Monday.

To protect the system over the weekend, Sorensen told his technical guys to disconnect the external line to the computer, a crude solution but the only one they could improvise on the spot. On Monday morning they began a marathon effort, the second in as many weeks, to design, write and erect a series of firewalls to ensure protection from a future hack. The project took most of that second week to complete, and final debugging and testing was finished late on Thursday evening. An incident-review committee was set up, but they waited to meet until the programmer was free to brief them on the nature of the problem. The result of that meeting, much to the relief of Sorensen and the entire staff of the technical department, was the decision to turn the problem over to the Denton City Police Department. Finding the hacker or hackers was now a police problem and two detectives, Chuck Harris and Ken Nesbit, were briefed for the job early on Friday, the twenty-sixth.

The investigators following up on the case were not initially concerned with the change to the tax roll information. It was a single illegal entry and it made no sense; that is, it did not seem to benefit the taxpayer or anybody else. The idea that it might have been a silly, childish joke did not occur to them. They were police officers and they viewed the hack as a criminal act, like breaking into someone's house or business. Even if nothing was stolen, the break-in was itself a crime, whether it made any sense or not.

From the phone company's search of their records, the officers knew that a local company, CompuNetPlus, a dial-up Internet service provider with a largely residential client base, was the probable source of the call they were looking for, and the police contacted the company on Friday afternoon. The manager proved to be very cooperative. The people at CompuNetPlus were not shocked to learn that a hacker had used their service to hack into the city's computer. They were far more aware of the hacker problem than were either the police or the city programmers now sweating over their system to block any further illicit access to their system.

Clients who log onto a server, whether by dial-up or high-speed continuous access, are tracked by their phone numbers, and thus easily identified. But once a client has logged on, the service provider has no further interest in the vast number of Internet connections its clients make. A fair number of clients had logged onto the system between 8:00 and 10:00 on Sunday evening, the fourteenth, almost two weeks earlier, the approximate time when the computer log said the changes had been made to the city's data file. The company could and did supply the police with the phone numbers and billing addresses for the clients in question, but it could not identify which specific client had hacked into the city's system. Identifying that specific number from the list they were given looked to the detectives like searching for the proverbial needle in a haystack. But as they began looking over the list, they saw that this particular haystack showed only one business address among a list of residential clients. The travel agent's business address stuck out like a sore thumb. Once again they had a lead and they followed up on it immediately.

The travel agent was more curious about the police visit than intimidated by it. No, she said, she had not used her office computer on Sunday evening two weeks ago or on any Sunday evening. Her father came to dinner every Sunday and the whole family was always there, and that was easily verified. But from the phone records the detectives knew that her phone line had been connected to her service provider on the fourteenth. She had no idea how that could be, but she did have a little mystery of her own. The answering machine on her business line had registered an incoming call on several Sunday evenings, and from the squeal on the answering machine she knew it had been a computer calling. Her system could recognize and route a signal to either the fax machine or the computer, and she was familiar with both sounds. She had called the number once and gotten a modem squeal for her troubles, but maybe it was a number they should check out? Perhaps it was connected to their case in some way.

She saw the puzzled look on the detectives' faces and explained that she had been harassed by an old boyfriend for some time and she had to get a court order to prevent him from calling her either here or at her home. The phone company monitored her lines and they provided the numbers of any calls she was concerned about. She thought she should check out the Sunday night calls and that's how she knew the number. She got it for them from her desk blotter, and the detectives left wondering if they were making progress or just going in circles.

Ken Nesbit ran the number by the phone company and it turned out to be the computer lab in a local high school. Interesting. Who would be using the school's computer lab on a Sunday evening? And more importantly, using it for what? None of it made any sense to either of them. The more information they had, the less they knew for sure.

Then they ran this new information past the manager at CompuNetPlus simply because they couldn't make sense of any of it. Ken explained that the call they were interested in had apparently come from someone in a high-school lab who called a travel agent's computer, which had then apparently called CompuNetPlus all by itself. Did that make any sense? The manager said it did. They had not run into that problem yet, but it was "on the radar" as he put it. Now that they knew it had happened, or appeared to have happened, they would have to figure out how to deal with it, and he thanked Ken for the "heads-up." He went on to explain that theoretically it was possible for one computer to call a second computer, read its list of passwords and use those and its Internet access number to dial into a server; and the server would record the call as coming from someone on its client list. Once logged onto a server, the hacker could go anywhere on the Internet because he still had control of his machine. So that would seem to suggest that someone in the school's computer lab was the hacker and it would also explain how he had gained access to the city's data files. The program he used to take control of a second machine would have to have a password cracker or some brute-force capability, and when it was through to the city's computer it would have called up its cracker program to break the passwords and get into its data files.

There was still time on Friday to visit the school, but they decided they wouldn't go near the computer lab for fear of alerting the hackers; besides, they had other leads to follow up on first. Since the calls came into the travel agent's office only on a

Sunday evening and the hack had been made on a Sunday evening, they asked for and got permission to place a tap on that phone line so the police would be alerted if the school hackers called again this Sunday evening. It was a stretch, but it seemed a reasonable step to take.

The request for a background check on the victim or target of an incident was routine and the results were waiting for them after lunch at the district station. The "victim" was a teacher. Not only did he have a degree in computer science, but he was also currently employed in the same school from which the hack had probably been made. In fact, he taught accounting courses in that same computer lab, so he would likely have keys for both the building and for the computer lab and probably unlimited access to both. Interesting stuff. There was obviously a connection here, but it was too early to say exactly what it was.

A little more legwork on Friday and a veritable avalanche of data descended on them. Chuck called the school to establish that Mr. Scrivner was still employed there and to arrange a convenient time when they could have an informal chat with him. The secretary said yes, Scrivner was still employed at the school, but was a little vague about why he was not at work today. From the principal they learned that he was on suspension, and at that point they made an appointment with the principal for later that afternoon, to get a little more information about Mr. Scrivner and his problems at work.

It was while they were on their way to the school that a patrolman called them to say he had stopped by Scrivner's apartment as they had requested. When no one answered the door, he had chatted with the nosy neighbour from across the hall. The neighbour told him about the electricity being cut off and the door locks being changed and that Mr. Scrivner had apparently just left without telling anybody that he was going away or even leaving a key with the building manager in case of an emergency.

The principal, Mr. Burden, confirmed to them that Scrivner was not at work today and explained why. It was the end of term and he had student exams to grade and report-card marks to make up, but none of this work had been done and Burden had suspended him pending a more formal hearing about his conduct. From the school secretary the detectives learned about Scrivner's financial troubles with the bank and his car being repossessed, and she confirmed what they already knew from the patrolman about his housing problems. The secretary didn't know where he was staying, but suggested that Bill Bird might, and found his address for them.

Chuck and Ken had just missed Bill Bird at school and they were now taking a break before deciding what to do next. Most of the time you have nothing to go on as you start an investigation, but suddenly they were drowning in facts. It was all related somehow, but none of it seemed to make much sense. What they needed now was time to write up and digest what they already knew before they could figure out where to go next. There was no reason to panic. Sorensen, the city's computer programmer, had assured them that he had the computer sealed up tight against a repeat of the initial entry. The tap on the travel agent's line could remain in place indefinitely, but it might never get another call from the school lab. They even had a recent photo of Scrivner supplied by the school from the yearbook shoot. But it was all speculation and surmise. They had no hard evidence that the hacker's call had even come from the school. Really, the only thing they needed to do, or at least the only thing it seemed logical to do, was find where Scrivner was staying and have a chat with him. Or would interviewing Scrivner be a smart idea until they knew what they needed to talk to him about? In the end they decided to call it a day and sort it all out in the morning.

The morning proved productive. Chuck wrote up what they had so far and, while it was far from conclusive, it did make interesting reading. Then they worked out their approach to Scrivner and decided to drop round to Bill Bird's apartment unannounced to see if Scrivner was staying there. When they knocked, it was Scrivner who answered the door, and he greeted them warily.

"Mr. Scrivner? I'm Detective Harris and this is my partner Detective Nesbit. Could we come in and chat with you for a minute?" Chuck pocketed his police identification and waited for permission to enter.

Scrivner nodded, but said nothing and moved toward the living room. They followed him and he gestured for them to sit. Then he asked the obvious question, "What's this all about?"

Chuck picked it up, following the approach they had worked out earlier that morning.

"It's about a computer glitch down at city hall that has really caused some headaches for a lot of people, and we think you are one of them. Apparently the computer screwed up a while ago and nobody noticed it until it had changed a lot of information in the tax records. The people in the city's tax department are not sure what happened, but they don't think this is just some hiccup in their computers. They think it was deliberate tampering with the tax information. Apparently a hacker got in and messed with the files, and if that is what happened, they want to know why. So they called us in and we're interviewing all of the people affected just to see if they've noticed anything unusual or been approached by anybody with some kind of story that might be a scam related to the changes. It's possible there might be a pattern here, a criminal con, and if so, we need to get right on it."

Chuck thought that sounded pretty good and apparently Scrivner did too, for he brightened up immediately and the story came pouring out like champagne from a warm bottle. "I know what you're talking about," he said, "and I am so glad to finally get a chance to tell someone about it, face to face. This thing's been a nightmare. It's like I've been carrying a boulder on my back for the last few days."

Chuck said nothing, but nodded encouragingly and waited for Scrivner to go on.

"I didn't know anything about the change of information in the tax files, but I guessed it was something like that. Things started going nuts for me on Tuesday morning. Can you believe," he said, "that the city cut off the electricity to my apartment at 7:30 in the morning with no warning or explanation or anything? And would you believe..."

Scrivner had waited for this chance since Tuesday and he didn't miss a thing. He catalogued every event, every inconvenience, every frustration and when he got to the conversation with Mr. Hefflendorf of the city's administration department, Ken snorted and stifled a laugh. He looked sheepishly at Chuck and said, "Well, this Hefflendorf sounds a lot like Perkins over in payroll." And the three of them shared a brief chuckle.

They thanked Scrivner for his candour and his time, assured him that they would pass his concerns on to the city for their consideration and left. They stopped for lunch and reviewed their impressions of Scrivner, now that they had met him and heard his story. Nothing made any sense. Scrivner seemed much more like the victim of a crime than the perpetrator of one. If there was any scam or criminal plot or any other design to the disruption caused by this computer break-in, neither of them could see what it was. But that wouldn't stop them from calling Scrivner on some pretext or other Sunday evening, just to make sure they knew where he was in the event another attempt was made to get into the city's computer system.

Eric Sorensen would also be in his office Sunday evening. The department managers had all been told not to contact the computer over the weekend, and he changed the passwords just to make sure none of them blundered into the system in spite of his warnings. Now he almost hoped the dweeb would try again, because he wanted to see how well his firewalls would work. No, he decided, he definitely wanted this guy to try again, because what he really wanted was to nail his hide to the wall. Of course, Chuck and Ken would be on duty, too, and Sorensen would call them just as soon as a call was detected. But they all knew it wouldn't be enough. It was all they could do, but they didn't have the sophisticated equipment to do a line-trace in real time. And there was no way the phone company was going to man their data centre on the off chance that an important call might be coming through sometime over the weekend.

As it turned out, they had no need of such sophisticated equipment to identify the hackers or to locate them. Jeff and Willard would volunteer that information themselves.

Immediately after they had changed Mr. Scrivner's tax file two weeks earlier, even before Scrivner had a clue what was in store for him, Jeff knew they were in way over their heads. He assumed Willard understood that too, but with Willard there was no way to know for sure. They didn't talk about going back to the lab the following Sunday, November 21st, but when Willard came over to his house, Jeff suggested that they stay in and watch videos instead of going to school, and Willard agreed. Apparently Willard was as scared as Jeff was to go back into the school and use the computers again, at least for this Sunday.

They were halfway through their second video, a horror flick that did nothing to lift the sense of gloom they both shared, when Willard asked Jeff if he thought they should tell Mr. Scrivner what they had done. Jeff's eyes bulged and the salsa dripped off the chip he was eating. Being scared they would get caught was one thing, but going to Mr. Scrivner and telling him that they had been breaking into the school and using the computer lab for months and that they had probably screwed up his tax file? That was too much for Jeff, and he said so. Willard continued sipping his Coke as though he hadn't heard Jeff's reply. It was a stupid idea, Jeff said, because nothing had happened yet and maybe nothing would. The city had probably found the error and just fixed Mr. Scrivner's tax file themselves, so there was no reason to tell him anything. Then Jeff asked Willard if he wanted to end up in Burden's office explaining to him about the computers. Mr. Scrivner would have to tell Burden what a pair of idiots they had been, and Burden would make them explain to their parents how they came to have a key to the computer lab and what they had been doing on Sunday evenings for the past few months. That settled the matter, and there it rested until Tuesday the 23rd, when really weird things started happening to Mr. Scrivner.

The D command and the computer's stubborn refusal to let them quit the program until it got a date had come back to haunt them, and now it made perfect sense. They watched the mess they had created spiral out of control, but they were helpless to stop it. This time they really had killed Mr. Scrivner, at least as far as the computer was concerned, and somehow that was the cause of all his problems. They would have tried to reverse the error if they had not been paralyzed with fear, but now it was too late. The school had put in a motion-detector alarm system covering the hallways and stairwells, and they were testing it this weekend. The idea was that if burglars or vandals got into the school by smashing a ground-floor window, as they occasionally did, they would set off the alarm the minute they opened the door and entered the hallway. They always went looking for stuff to steal, and this very cheap alarm system would effectively put a stop to the illegal entries once and for all.

So, the computer lab was closed to them. They could still use the shim to get into the classroom on the ground floor, but they couldn't get from the ground floor to the computer lab without setting the alarm off. Then Willard, showing more initiative than Jeff would have given him credit for, figured that if they could climb up onto the wood shop's storage shed, they could get onto the flat roof at the back of the school. Then they could simply walk across the roof to the windows of the computer lab on the second floor. It was a good bet that one of the windows could be opened with the shim and they would have direct access to the lab from the first-floor roof. They would have no need to unlock the door or to be in the halls. All they wanted was to work in the lab; who would ever know about it? In fact, with the alarm system in place, they'd be more secure in the lab now than before they put the alarm system in. And Willard proved to be right. Getting in was just as easy as he had said it would be.

And so it was that, while Mr. Scrivner spent Sunday the 28th, suspended from his job and dreading what Monday and a meeting with the superintendent might bring, Willard was back working on his computer games, and Jeff was sweating over the problem of how to get back into the city's computer. But it was hopeless. Snoop and Scoop couldn't cope with the new firewalls the programmers had erected. Jeff finally admitted defeat, exited the program, shut his machine down and went to get some pizza before Willard ate it all.

They ate the cold pizza and finished off all six of their Cokes. Then Willard had to go for a pee. Jeff looked up as Willard went to the door, but before he could yell a warning, Willard opened it and stepped out into the hall. The lights flashed, the bell rang and an alarm louder than the intruder alert on the starship Enterprise let loose all at once. They fell all over themselves trying to get the window open and get out onto the roof. Jeff had to hang onto Willard to keep him from jumping off the roof to the concrete drive twelve feet below and he forced him to climb back down onto the shed roof and down to the ground. The police were coming around the back of the building before they reached the ground.

When they saw the police, they were so scared they were speechless for about a minute, then they confessed to everything. They begged for mercy, convinced the police had been lying in wait all along to catch them red-handed and drag them off to jail. The police officers, both long-time veterans, took a few minutes outside the car to stop laughing before informing the pair that they were under arrest and that, yes, they were being taken to jail.

Chuck and Ken were alerted by Eric Sorensen that an attempted hack was in progress and instantly Ken was back on the line to check up on Scrivner. It was the third time he had called and he had run out of excuses to explain why he was calling to speak to Scrivner with apparently no purpose other than to assure himself that Scrivner was at home. Scrivner knew the first two calls were fishy, but this time Ken blurted out that they had the hackers in custody and on their way to the district station, and that it might be useful, although he did not say how, if Scrivner would come down and just be on hand in case they needed him for something or other. It was phrased as an invitation, but he could see the red and blue lights of a patrol car flashing outside the building and the heavy tread of police boots were already sounding on the stairs before he hung up.

In fifteen minutes he was sitting outside an interview room with Chuck Harris and Ken Nesbit, watching as two small figures were bundled into the room on the other side of the one-way mirror. When the two big cops sat them down and moved away from them, Scrivner's jaw dropped open and he stared in disbelief. And then he laughed. The two detectives had been watching for some reaction from Scrivner, but laughter was not the reaction they were expecting.

The human brain is not supposed to be able to process that much complicated data in the time it takes to blink an eye, but Scrivner's did. One glance at Willard Ransom staring vacantly at himself in the mirror and Jeff Kershaw wiping his nose on his shirt sleeve, and it all made perfect sense.

Ken broke the silence and asked, "Do you know these kids, Mr. Scrivner?"

Scrivner opened his mouth, but nothing came out. How could he explain Willard and Jeff to this young policeman? Finally he said, "Oh yes, Officer, I know them."

Chuck was becoming agitated. He expected more from Scrivner and he didn't understand the way he was acting. "How do you know them?" he asked. "Like, are they students of yours or just kids you have met at school, or are they even students at your school? We need some answers, Mr. Scrivner. There are a lot of very tired people over at city hall who want to know what's going on. So lay it out for us. How do you know these kids and what is the connection between them and you?"

"I don't have the answers for you, Detective; that is, I do not have the hard facts you want, but I can guess what has been going on. In fact, now that I know Jeff and Willard are behind it, I can see exactly how it all happened. But I'll tell you this straight off. Whatever they did and however badly they screwed up the city's computer, I can assure you it wasn't a malicious act.

You won't be able to blame them for it. It would be like blaming a bull for destroying the china shop he just happened to wander through." Scrivner paused and then continued, "Come on. Let's get this all down on tape or something so I can go home. I'm tired, too. I'm so tired that I can't even enjoy the relief I should be feeling now that it's all over, but I will tomorrow and I expect I'll laugh about it then, too. But not now. So let's get my statement down on tape and then we can all go home to bed."

It took about an hour and Scrivner laid out the whole process, as he now understood it. He described what he had been through and he theorized what the boys had done to create this mess. He had no clue the boys had been using the lab, but they must have been. And he didn't find out about Snoop and Scoop until after the boys were questioned, but, again, he understood that some program like it would have been required to make the connection from the school lab to the Internet, for he knew Jeff and Willard could not have made that leap by themselves.

When their parents arrived, the sergeant in charge gave the boys a dressing-down before releasing them into the custody of their parents, with a reminder that they would very likely be facing charges after the Crown prosecutor had reviewed the tapes of the interview.

Several days later, Jeff and Willard and their parents were called to the Crown prosecutor's office to hear what charges they were going to face. The prosecutor had listened to Scrivner's tape, and by the time it finished she was ready to slice and dice the pair of them. Then she saw the interview with the boys and she had to rethink what to do with them. The arresting officers had described their behaviour at the time of their arrest and she could picture them as she read that report and watched the video of the interview. Willard was mumbling incoherently and Jeff was blubbering all over the table in the interview room. She saw no malicious intent in their actions. Besides, she had researched the law on computer crime and found it vague and unsatisfactory. The break-in at the school was more like a prank than a crime and, as far as she could tell, all they did when they got into the building was to carry on with much the same work they did in class after they had completed their day's assignment. What was the point of a criminal charge for that? The hack into the city's computer was a more serious matter, and the overtime bill was significant, but according to Sorensen, the city's programmer, it was a good wake-up call and it was money that the city would have spent anyway to do the programming they had now completed, and in record time.

However much inconvenience they may have caused, did they deserve to face criminal charges and would society benefit from giving them a criminal record? The parents, Kershaw and Ransom, had made an offer of compensation to Mr. Scrivner, the only person specifically injured by this prank, and he had accepted it immediately. If he had accepted a modest sum as full compensation for the inconvenience he had suffered from their foolishness, and if he could accept the kid's apologies as genuine expressions of regret, and if no one else had an axe to grind, why crucify the kids? Besides, from what she had gathered about the school board's intentions, there was a good chance they would both be expelled, and that would likely cost them their graduation. That seemed to her a far harsher penalty than any court would have imposed for an act of childish foolishness. There was, she decided, no point in criminal charges, but she would ream them out, and she knew that even some police officers flinched when she was in full stride and raking them over the coals.

Once the facts were all known, the city moved with commendable speed to clear things up for Mr. Scrivner. It took two days for the electrical department to unseal the service and turn the power back on in his condo. And it took another day before they gave him the keys to his new locks. There was some question whether he would have to pay for the locksmith's time, but the mayor intervened and the maintenance department simply ate that cost themselves. The bank moved much faster than the city and the moment they were officially informed of the screwup, they released their hold on his accounts and all of the scheduled transactions were processed. Someone from the bank's public relations department personally called the finance company to explain about the missed payment and to assure them that Scrivner was as reliable as ever. The next morning his car simply appeared in its usual parking slot at school, without Scrivner even having to call to find out where it was.

Scrivner exchanged a few choice words with Principal Burden when he came back to work on Monday, and the superintendent had to mediate between them. Report cards had been issued without his marks, pending his completion of the marking and grading of all his students. No one, other than the principal, had doubted that Scrivner would finish his work as soon as his problems had worked themselves out. The superintendent did some checking and the general consensus among the senior administrative staff was that Burden had to go. The superintendent suggested to Burden that he might like to take early retirement at the end of this semester. They did a little dancing back and forth, but it was a done deal as soon as the issue was raised. It really suited both of them. The principal was due to retire anyway, and the superintendent found enough in the slush fund to offer him a nice little incentive package to ensure his speedy agreement. The vice-principal moved up to take the principal's job, Bill Bird applied for and got the vice-principal's job immediately, and in the fall Scrivner would be moved into the computer lab as full-time computer teacher, to the satisfaction of students and staff alike.

That left only the problem of Jeff and Willard and how the board of education resolved to punish them. Scrivner requested permission to address the board on the topic of a suitable punishment for them, and he was largely responsible for encouraging the board to reverse its decision to expel both of them. His argument was that here were two students who had barely passed a subject from grade one until they had found the computer. In this, their graduating year, they had passing grades in all subjects and outstanding marks in every computer course they were allowed to take. Teachers spend the whole of their working lives attempting to motivate students to work as hard as these two were obviously working now, and he felt strongly that expulsion was inappropriate in this case.

He presented the board with an alternative proposal to impose 200 hours of community service on them in place of expulsion. They would serve their time after school in the accounting department at city hall, where they would come to understand the inconvenience they had caused these people. He had done his homework well and he knew that most courts did not give young offenders, especially first-time offenders like Jeff and Willard, sentences much tougher than this. The memo he presented to the board was endorsed by Sorenson for the city, recommended by the Crown prosecutor and presented and argued by Scrivner himself, the person most seriously effected by this childish prank. The board was sandbagged. They accepted the proposal without a dissenting vote.

There, before a full meeting of the board of education, with their parents in attendance as spectators, the boys were called to account for their actions. The chairman went on about their "criminal behaviour" for about half an hour before laying Scrivner's compromise on them. They hung their heads in shame. Then, again with their parents in attendance, they had to face the superintendent, who also chewed them out about their "criminal behaviour" before laying a suitable suspension on them. They felt lower than worm slime. They dreaded coming back to school after their suspensions were finished, and cringed at the thought of everybody laughing at them for being so stupid.

But it was worse than they had imagined. It was all anybody was talking about. Suddenly they were very cool dudes. They had breached the city's computer security system, and everybody wanted to know what they were going to do next. They were surrounded by girls who wanted to carry their books, and girls called them up and wanted to go out with them. They wanted to run their fingers through Willard's wiry hair, and polish Jeff's shiny bald spot. Suddenly being the only boy in school with a receding hairline was very sexy. Which was all fine and dandy, but all this unexpected attention from the female population of the school was very disruptive. Girls don't talk about stuff geeks like Jeff and Willard are interested in—and all that giggling! It was just too much for either of them.

Fortunately, they were off to the city's accounting department to serve their community-service obligations most afternoons and that proved to be an experience they would both remember. Jeff was assigned to work with a geek in programming who was analyzing Snoop and Scoop in order to write a blocking program against it in case it ever showed up again, and they worked very well together. Willard, initially as out of place in the accounting department as a turnip in an Easter egg hunt, talked someone in the programming department into letting him play with the logo design, and before the end of their community time he had perfected a sort of reverse explosion for the logo on the Internet site. It started with roiling clouds of various colours and then resolved itself into the city's logo on a background of pastel shades. It was too far-out for the city fathers, but it was an impressive piece of programming, and Eric Sorenson himself called Willard in to tell him so.

They knew what Scrivner had done for them. None of them ever mentioned it again, but for the rest of the term they dropped into the computer lab after school now and then, just to let him know what they were doing at city hall.

Miss Wilson Says Goodbye

Miss Wilson unlocked her classroom door for the last time. She had been teaching elementary school for thirty-two years. She could have taken retirement several years earlier, but she had been waiting for one last episode in her life to resolve itself; and now it had. Tomorrow was the start of the Christmas break, and today she would say goodbye to the children.

Retirement isn't always the cause for celebration that young people think it is. It means different things to different people. To Muriel Wilson it was like abandoning something of herself. For many years, her grade one classes had been the only family she had known. She realized that she had depended on them, as they had depended on her over the years. In resigning, she was cutting herself adrift from a lifetime of caring for one generation of children after another. She had never married. These would be the last children she would ever know, and she would miss them terribly. And that knowledge had tempered the excitement she felt as this day approached.

Muriel had tendered her resignation to take effect at the beginning of the Christmas holiday. She had begun the process of applying for her retirement pension at the beginning of the school year and she had quietly evaded all attempts by the staff to find out what she was planning to do in her retirement. Just how well she had maintained her privacy became obvious to her from a remark she overheard from the staff room. Muriel was about to enter for lunch when she overheard Mrs. Olivette, the grade four teacher just back from maternity leave, holding forth for the benefit of the other teachers in the room.

"You know how you can tell when someone's been teaching grade one for thirty years?" she asked. "When they talk in printing. Watch Muriel when she is trying to make a point. You can almost hear the chalk scraping on the blackboard while she thinks. Grade one can be hazardous to your mental health."

A chorus of quiet laughter died as Muriel entered the room, and she was careful to give no indication that she had heard the remark. It was really quite a funny remark, and yes, she was very precise when she spoke. Perhaps you actually do take on some of the mannerisms of the people you spend your life with, and she had spent her whole adult life with small children. It didn't matter. She knew herself very well, but the remark had hurt, and it came so close to her resignation date that some of the staff would undoubtedly think that dissatisfaction with her position, or the vague implication of the joke, that some of the staff thought that it was time for her to go, was a factor in her decision to retire at this time.

Never mind, she thought, as she automatically put her jacket in the cupboard and placed her purse in the bottom drawer of her desk, as she had each working day of her life for thirty-two years. What other people thought was their business, and besides, she had a more pressing matter to deal with. Mr. Fluffy was dead.

Swen Jorgensen, the janitor, stuck his head into the room to ask if there was anything she needed. He looked at her for a moment and then said, "Well Muriel, what's up? You don't look so good." He was puzzled for a moment. She was obviously preoccupied with something.

She smiled absently, then gestured toward the rabbit lying on the bottom of his cage.

"I'm fine Swen. It's the rabbit. He must have died last night. I'll have to dispose of him before the children come in and find him like that."

"Oh, poor old fella. I'll take him away." Swen stepped into the room, but hesitated, sensing that Muriel did not want him to move the rabbit.

She shook her head and smiled at him. "No. Thank you, Swen, but I think I have to take care of this myself." Someone would have to deal with the rabbit, but if the children were to see the janitor carting him away, they would never forgive her.

"Well, if you're sure," he said, lingering a moment. "But I don't mind, you know." If Muriel said she would look after it, then that's how it would be. She wasn't one to change her mind easily.

She shooed him out of the room with a tilt of her head, and he grinned back a "Yah, sure," as he left.

Muriel made her way to the office and asked the secretary to call Bill Kenton, the science teacher, to come down to the grade one room. She stood quietly while the secretary made the adjustments to the PA system and called his room.

Bill Kenton answered the summons from the office with his usual bad-tempered, "Yeah? What?"

The PA system broadcast all answers loud enough for everyone in the office to hear, and Kenton knew that. He simply didn't care.

"Mr. Kenton," the secretary said, adjusting the volume a little lower, "Muriel would be grateful if you would come down to her room as soon as possible. She says she has a problem she needs your help with. What shall I tell her?"

"Now what? If Harold let the salamander loose in her classroom again, I'll kill that kid!"

Muriel heard, smiled and shook her head. The secretary simply repeated Muriel's request that he come to her room as soon as possible.

"Well, look. Tell her I can't come before period two. I've got a spare then and I'll drop in when I can. If it's an emergency, let Swen take care of it. I don't know why she thinks I...Well, just tell her I'll be down when I can."

Bill Kenton was known to suffer from a good deal of stress. Muriel knew he tended to drink socially to unwind, and it appeared he had been using a little too much again. He usually did just before the holidays. Mornings were rather difficult for him. He was less than half her age, and she could understand the struggles he was having. Teaching was changing. Children had so many more social problems now than they'd had when she was young. Adults had problems, too, like Bill Kenton's drinking. It never showed in his teaching though; he functioned very well in the classroom and he was popular with the kids. Still, she mused, it would be better for his career if he learned to curb his outbursts a little.

Back in her room, she cast about looking for something to throw over the rabbit cage. She took the name card, Mr. Fluffy, from the holder on the side of the cage and put it face down on the chalk ledge under the front blackboard. It was already 8:30 a.m. and the children would arrive any minute. She hoped Mr. Kenton would change his mind and come down sooner, because she could not have the rabbit in the classroom all day. It was the last day of school, the beginning of Christmas holidays. There would be the concert at 10:00 and early dismissal at 12:00. Students would be coming and going out of the upper grades all day long. He could easily come down at any time and no one would criticize him for being out of his classroom for a few minutes.

"Yeah, Muriel. You wanted to see me?" Bill Kenton, brusque as ever, stood in the doorway, impatient to be gone. But he had come, and she was grateful for it.

"Oh, Bill, we have a problem, I'm afraid. It's the rabbit." As she said this, she removed the cover and opened the cage door.

He looked in. The rabbit was on its side, stretched out to its full length, with its feet pressing the bars at the front and back of the cage. He poked the furry body. It was an angora, and the fur was very thick and heavy, hence the name Mr. Fluffy. The children had loved holding him and watching him hop about the room picking up bits of celery or carrots, on the regular occasions when Muriel would permit him to come out. She took care of his grooming and cleaning herself, always in the evening after the children had gone home. In such a confined area the fur tended to mat, and she made sure the cage was always clean and that the rabbit was well turned out each day for the children to see and appreciate.

"Well he's dead, Muriel. He has bit the bullet, gone to his reward. What can I tell you? Don't make soup, he's been gone too long." Bill Kenton turned to her and with a shrug of his shoulders added, "Er, was there something else?"

She was not offended. He was not as difficult as he appeared to be. He was just unhappy. He wanted to do good things in his classroom, but they had cut his budget again for the fifth straight year. How much real science can you do with a handful of old Pyrex glassware and the scratched stuff in his lab? Most of it was hand-me-downs from the high school, and every time Bill asked for more equipment, the teachers up there made him feel like a beggar, which, of course, he was. Still, he had taken enough science courses at night and in the summers to qualify for certification as a specialist in science—elementary and secondary—and that was something many of the high school teachers had yet to accomplish.

She smiled at him and assured him she knew it was dead. But the children loved the rabbit and they would want to know, even if they never said so in so many words, that she had some other authority for pronouncing him dead. Bill Kenton was Mr. Science at the school and his was the closest thing to an expert opinion the children could hope to get. Besides that, Bill was the school's rep on the environmental committee for the county. You don't just throw a dead animal in the garbage anymore. There are very strict guidelines on how to deal with a carcass now, and Bill would know what to do. Still, he did not volunteer any comment past his initial one. She had to ask him what to do with the carcass and only then did he seem to understand what was required. She held a garbage bag ready. He lifted the rabbit and slipped it carefully into the bag, took it from her and left. She removed the dirty paper, put it in the garbage, replaced it with fresh newspaper and closed the cage. She did not cover it again. There was no point.

Poor Mr. Fluffy, she thought and blinked away a tear. She always felt a sense of loss when a pet died, but there would be tears enough when the children came in and found the cage empty.

She plugged in the lights on the little Christmas tree set up on a small table in the corner of the room. There was a large tree in the gym, but the children only saw that tree for a little while during the entire season and they had enjoyed her little one over the years. They came in in a flurry of noise and happy confusion. It was a party day, and they knew it. They were so hyper that she should have quieted them down and asserted discipline over them immediately. Under normal circumstances, with such a start to the day, they would be almost out of control, but she knew that would not be a problem today.

Someone noticed Mr. Fluffy was not in his cage, and the noise level began to fall immediately. She said nothing, but waited for the noise to settle. Before she could say anything, the bell sounded, and the morning exercises were on the PA. The children stood quietly, but as soon as the music and talking were over, they demanded to know where Mr. Fluffy was. She told them the truth with no condescension to their age. The rabbit was dead. Mr. Kenton had come and confirmed it. There was no mistake. He had taken Mr. Fluffy away. All things that live eventually die. Mr. Fluffy was very old for a rabbit. Every child in the school had known him, and his time had just come.

It was typical of her way of looking at life that she did not lecture them on how they should feel. She did not, for instance, tell them that they should not feel bad because he had had a good long life. Nor did she tell them that the rabbit had gone to a better life. She believed in a loving God, but she would let the children make up their own minds about the nature of a world where, no matter how much you love something or someone, you must eventually lose it to death—its death or your own.

Then there were the tears. She shared in them. She took a tissue and passed the box to the children, who all took one in turn. When she wiped her eyes and blew her nose, it was a signal for the rest of the class to do the same, and one by one they did. She placed the small classroom garbage container out in front of her desk and dropped her tissue into it. The children followed suit. One of the children saw the sign, Mr. Fluffy, lying face down on the chalk ledge. He knew what it was even with the name face down. She would put it in the garbage eventually, but not just yet. He made a suggestion and, after a moment, she agreed.

She took a bit of tape, attached it to the back of the sign and hung it on one of the branches of the little Christmas tree. It was totally out of proportion to the other ornaments on the tree and made no sense as a decoration, but why not? Hanging up the sign was too much for some of the children and they began to cry again, but Muriel Wilson was having none of that. They had had their cry and drenched one tissue apiece, and that was enough. She ignored the tears and the sniffles and called for the children to form a semicircle for the last rehearsal of their carol medley before the concert. And that was that.

Death, sorrow, grieving, regret, acceptance, accommodation and, finally, the joy of living. In fifteen minutes, Miss Wilson had taught her grade one class a lesson in successful living that they would later remember in times of stress in their own lives.

Muriel had had her share of grief and grieving and she had known some bitter disappointments in her own life, as well. It had been her mother's ill health following her father's sudden death that had prompted Muriel to move into an apartment in the area to be nearby, and for several years she had continued to make the long drive to her former school—Meadowvale

Elementary. But twelve years ago, a grade one position came open here at Holy Name Elementary, and Muriel finally had the opportunity to enter the separate school system; she was glad she had. She had always enjoyed the traditions of her church and she was particularly grateful at this time of year that the separate system still celebrated the Christmas season with the re-enactment of the story of Christmas in a concert that the children and the community enjoyed so much.

That tradition had changed in the public system and was beginning to change even before she left. She wasn't sure if Meadowvale was still permitted to have a Christmas concert, but she was glad Holy Name did. The public system was under pressure to drop all ceremonies that might be considered Christian, though how Rudolph, Santa or Frosty the Snowman reflected Christianity was hard for Muriel to see. She had grown up looking forward to Christmas and enjoying the Christmas concert and she still did, despite the work and effort it required to make it a success. She felt there should be some kind of a public celebration to end the first half of the school year, otherwise children would look forward to the break only as a temporary reprieve from the drudgery of classes. To Muriel it seemed those schools that chose to present a winter fest celebration or a drama club presentation as a high note on which to end the year were doing something intrinsically good for student morale. Student morale was not as big a problem in elementary school as it was in high school, but the concert was still one of the highlights of the year for her, and her grade ones would steal the show. They might not remember what they sang, but they would remember being proud of the applause they got for their singing, and she wanted them to have that as their memory of her last day with them.

"Good morning, everyone," the principal's voice boomed over the PA. "Would teachers of grades five and six classes take their students down to the gym now, please, and would the rest of the staff hold their classes until they are called. Thank you."

Muriel set her class to cleaning the crumbs of the treats they had been eating off their desktops and instructed them to go looking for bits of paper around their desks to put in the trash. There weren't any, of course, but now that some students were moving to the gym, they would all be excited to go too, and Muriel had no intention of lining them up too early, only to stand screaming at them to be quiet.

"Would teachers of grades two, three and four take their classes down to the gym now, please." This time it was the secretary calling over the PA, because by now the principal would be in the gym schmoozing with the important people and praying that nobody set off the fire alarm and that the stage curtains worked smoothly for the performance.

Muriel kept the children busy organizing their personal stuff to take home and setting it out on their desktops while she did a quick inspection of heads to make sure there wasn't a stray candy cane stuck where it shouldn't be. Then she called them all to attention, had them sit up straight and told them what a wonderful class they were and how well they were all going to do when they were called to sing at the concert. As if on cue, the PA cut in and the secretary finally called them down to the gym so the concert could begin.

The grade five and six classes had been lined up on the stage for a good ten minutes waiting for the curtain to open, and they were getting restless. There were angels and shepherds and wise men in abundance, and the balance of the classes were standing on risers, ready to play out their parts as required. Bill Kenton had lined his kids up and threatened them with dire consequences if they did not pay attention to Miss Harcourt, the prompter offstage, while he was absent. Bill had the Santa suit and would be watching from the back of the gym until it was time to put on the coat and beard and come running in with the usual sack of goodies. Before leaving them, he had singled out the likely troublemakers and fixed each individually with a warning glance, eyeball to eyeball.

But Harold, the kid Bill Kenton had suspected of letting the salamander loose in Muriel's classroom, was as good as gold. Too good, in fact. He had brought a water pistol and waited to use it until Leslie Watson was singing her solo in the pageant. He was planning to blast her, but at the last moment he lost his nerve. However, he did manage to soak Dwayne Jensen, standing next to him, in an underhand shot invisible to the audience, and as luck would have it, in the crotch of his pants. The girls beside Dwayne saw it and giggled. Dwayne was soaked and it looked like he had wet himself. Leslie heard the giggling behind her and thought the kids were laughing at her. She limped on for a few more bars and then burst into tears.

The prompter was at a loss to know what to do and was quite out of her depth. She was Muriel Wilson's replacement, just 23, starting her first teaching job and faced with a disaster she could barely comprehend. She started to hyperventilate. How do you get a singer to stop blubbering and start singing again? She was totally focused on Leslie and had not registered the quiet giggling until now, assuming, as Leslie had, that Leslie was the object of the distraction infecting the kids on the risers. Dwayne, by now red as a beet, decided that he did not care what happened while shepherds watched their flocks by night, or even if it was his turn to call out a message of peace on earth and goodwill to men. Harold must die! He turned to face Harold, gathered up his shepherd's crook and beaned him with a resounding "crack."

Harold was shocked. It had simply never occurred to him that quiet, easygoing Dwayne would attack him on stage, in front of an entire audience of parents, the rest of the school and even the people in suits from the county office, who intimidated everybody, including the principal.

Harold was hurt, but not mortally wounded. It's still a subject of some debate whether Dwayne remembered that the shepherds' crooks were only layers of newspaper held together with a bit of glue or if he thought, as quite a few in the audience obviously did, that the thing was made of solid wood. In any event,

Harold fell off the bench on which he and the rest of the boys were standing, a drop of only a foot or so. As he fell, however, his crook made contact with the wings of an angel standing in front of him and completely denuded her of her heavenly apparel. Leslie Watson, blubbering in her embarrassment but, like a seasoned trouper in a Broadway play, determined to carry on regardless, was suddenly joined in her wailing by Megan Pollick, the now wingless angel. Casting Megan as an angel must surely rank as one of the most monstrous examples of miscasting in all of theatrical history. She stomped the wings to shapeless sheets of crumpled paper and then joined Dwayne in seeking revenge on Harold, the villain of the piece, while the assembled adults—audience and teachers alike—sat for a full minute, not really comprehending the mayhem unfolding on the stage.

By now the broken crooks revealed the nature of their construction and their ultimate harmlessness. Dwayne's feverish thrashing at Harold's head with the fast-unravelling crook was seen by most in the audience as very funny. However, spurred more by fury than embarrassment, Megan looked about for something with which to aid Dwayne in finishing Harold off once and for all. Her glance revealed only the manger and the Christ child within easy reach. The manger was too heavy. The Christ child would have to do. She snatched up the doll by one leg and let fly at Harold, then hit Dwayne a glancing blow by mistake, sending the missile sailing across the stage and into the audience.

The roar of the crowd was deafening, and only then did a few teachers rise to their feet and rush toward the stage. The rest of the cast joined the fracas in one or another of the only two options open to them. The girls wailed; the boys fell off the bench—some forward, some backward, but all in total disarray. Punching and ineffectual hitting broke out all over the stage, to the absolute horror of the two grade six teachers who, until now, had stood by, too stunned to take in what was happening. Finally they waded in, pulling the boys apart, often with a little more force than was necessary. Bill Kenton, already wearing the black plastic boots and pants of the Santa suit, rushed up the three steps of the stage and added his bellowing to the general uproar.

In the midst of the melee, Muriel Wilson stood up, clapped her hands together as she would have in her class on a day only slightly noisier than usual, and instantly silenced both the audience and children alike.

"Grade one would like to sing some Christmas carols they have been practicing," was all she said. Her class stood on cue where they were on the gym floor, turned to face the audience and waited for the signal to start singing. Mrs. Underhill, the flustered music teacher who had been sitting at the piano all this time, was wringing her hands in despair. She looked at Muriel, who was waiting for her attention, as she would have waited for a child in a temper tantrum, and when she had it, Muriel gave her a nod to begin. But the carefully prepared script of musical selections was now out of order and quite useless, and Mrs. Underhill was as likely to improvise as a gerbil in an exercise wheel.

"What shall I play?" she asked in a desperate whisper that could be heard all the way to the back of the gym.

"Anything," said Muriel smiling, waiting, holding her gaze, knowing that if they lost eye contact, the lady was lost.

With that simple command, Mrs. Underhill was fine again. She started the introduction to the grade three play which, although a sprightly little number, had no words and was intended only to introduce a troupe of dancing elves and fairies. Muriel stood her ground. The children held hands and looked at her. She reassured them with a smile, and then, because it was a very short piece, waited patiently for the music teacher to finish. When she did, Muriel spoke very loudly, both for her benefit and that of the audience.

"We will start with 'Silent Night'."

They started with "Silent Night." The children picked it up in ragged chorus. The audience joined in, on her invitation, with the second verse. Her class did not know the second verse, so they sang the first verse again, but with considerably more confidence the second time around. The blending was like a descant in some modern rendition of the ancient carol. The grade six students on stage, in a remarkable show of unity for two factions so recently at war, picked up the tune and sang either the first or second verse, or possibly just hummed the familiar melody.

"We will sing 'Oh Come All Ye Faithful'."

They sang "Oh Come All Ye Faithful." Then they sang "The First Noel" and "Jingle Bells" and "Rudolph" and "Here Comes Santa Claus" and on and on for about fifteen minutes, with the little grade ones acting as though they did this sort of thing all the time. Then Bill Kenton, in considerably better humour than one might have expected, came rushing in with a flurry of "Ho, Ho, Hos," this time complete with Santa suit, coat and hat, and the requisite large white beard.

He gave out treats to all the good little boys and girls. Eventually, he turned to the assembled company on stage and asked them if they, too, had been good all year. No one said a word. When he turned to the audience and said, "Well, at least they haven't killed anybody in the last half hour," they broke into a roar of laughter and applause.

There were the appropriate closing words, and everyone was suitably shocked to hear of Miss Wilson's impending retirement. She was treated to a standing ovation by audience and children alike. Then, suddenly, it was all over.

For years the closing ritual of the school had been to finish the final day with a coffee or a drink over at the principal's house shortly after an early dismissal. It was there, with all the staff in attendance, that the principal made his presentation to her on behalf of the staff. There were some funny gifts, things such as people who have known each other for a long time are likely to give on such an occasion. There was the card, the very big "Happy Retirement" card, with several hundred signatures on it that she would keep and treasure for the rest of her life. There was a coffee mug with the inscription, "Welcome to the Rest of your life," even though everyone knew she didn't drink coffee. There was a shawl for her to wrap herself in as she sat in her rocker on her front balcony while all the rest of them were working.

But the shawl was a practical joke that instantly quieted the group. It had seemed very funny in the staff room, but now, draped around her shoulders as she in fact sat in a rocking chair, it seemed a very cruel joke. She was not in the least offended, however. She smiled, folded the shawl carefully and put it back in its box. She rose, pushed the chair back and smiled at them again, as she must have smiled on generations of her students.

"Thank you for your gifts and your kind words. And especially the shawl. I may find use for it immediately. Not in a rocking chair, however, because we leave on a Caribbean cruise the day after tomorrow, and I expect the deck chairs will be quite chilly at night."

The general clamour broke out immediately. We? Had she said, we?

Yes, she had. She'd been keeping company for five years now, and no, she was not surprised that no one knew that. They would have married several years ago, but he was not free then. He was free now, and that had prompted her resignation.

There were a number of things about her private life she doubted that they knew. For instance, none of them would know that she now owned the East View Towers Estates, where she lived. She had bought it eight years ago with the small legacy her parents had left her. It was not an elaborate building, but it was in great demand as a building site for commercial development. She had finished paying for it some five years ago and taken a small mortgage on it, and then she and her partner had gone together on the purchase of an industrial site that required no maintenance but which provided an excellent tax write-off against their rental income. Earlier in the week, the final papers had been signed on the sale of both properties, and now they were free to do as they wished.

They were all talking at once, but the sound of a horn outside interrupted the chatter. She leaned on the couch and brushed back the drape to wave at the driver. She had, she said, an announcement to make. She was going to donate a small sum of money to the school. They were not rich, but they had enough interest on the investments coming in so that, together with both of their pensions, she had to think about things like tax write-offs, and she could qualify for a credit of more than half the value of the gift she would make to the school. They had decided on five thousand dollars. She hoped the money would be used to buy equipment for the science room, and she wanted them to consider putting in some sort of enclosure for pets, where the children could keep a few rabbits and guinea pigs and such, but with space for them to run around in now and then.

When she was finished, she made her goodbyes in her usual dignified, unhurried way. Then she glided down the walk, in uncharacteristically lighthearted fashion, to join the janitor, her janitor, Swen Jorgensen, in the car.

~

About The Author

Ed Petersen left school early to help out with family expenses, an obligation the children of immigrant parents have traditionally accepted. He worked in retail sales, transportation and eventually became a general contractor. He paid his own way through university, following his interests rather than a specific career path. He studied theology in a degree program for several years before completing a degree in history at Sir Wilfred Laurier University, eventually taking education at the University of Toronto and the University of Western Ontario. He completed numerous professional development courses and, in later years, returned to university for further study in classical philosophy and history.

Ed began his career as a history teacher in Ontario. He accepted a position as Head of History after two years of experience and remained in Ontario for a number of years, teaching and administering a history department. He continued his career in Alberta as a social studies teacher and later moved into language arts, computer programming and computer literacy as the needs of the timetable in a small school dictated. He is currently a leading salesman for one of the largest publishing houses in Canada.

Ed lives in Calgary with his wife Betty and they enjoy a close relationship with their three adult children, now scattered abroad from Calgary to Vancouver to Japan.

~